FRIENDS MAKE THE BEST ENEMIES!

FRIENDS MAKE THE BEST ENEMIES!

Al-quan Mclendon

FRIENDS MAKE THE BEST ENEMIES!

iUniverse books may be ordered through booksellers or by contacting:

iUniverse
1663 Liberty Drive
Bloomington, IN 47403
www.iuniverse.com
1-800-Authors (1-800-288-4677)

ISBN: 978-1-5320-1893-0 (sc)
ISBN: 978-1-5320-1894-7 (e)

Library of Congress Control Number: 2017903478

Print information available on the last page.

iUniverse rev. date: 08/31/2018

ACKNOWLEDGMENT

I'm indebted to many individuals who have help me with the creation of this book, special thank you to my mother Vanessa, when I first told you I was writing you pushed me to do more than just short stories I sent to you and always believed in me know matter what I wanted to do and you never gave up on me Another special thanks to a woman who has been more than Big cousin to me you are a mother to me also thanks for the footwork you put in "To my son remember your Daddy loves you" Thank you to all my brothers and sisters, Bayez it ain't over never lay down, I told you I was going to take us to another level on these FOOLS and this is not it either I'm putting something else together and it's not a book Popz thanks "Jerome", Kintahe thanks for pushing me also what you tell me? I'm two steps ahead of them and they four step behind. Much love to all my cousins can't forget about the family.

Shout out to Jazz I know you would have bodied me if I did not say your name thanks for the help also, Tabjah you was the first person to try to get the book published for me you're a TRUE friend you never changed up on me and I love you for that.

Jabb, I love you lil bruh hold it up, Teairra all I'm going to say is you already know To my 20th Ave Boyz us as always much love

Much love to my P-town Boyz car wash one and two, shout out to King Ku-Fu, Riq, Hak, D-money, Maloney, Brother Reff, Baby, Park-Trub, Bob, Moby Head, Keefee, Kane, Mooka, YB

Rip to my Boyz, S4,Hoffa, Duke, through me y'all live on I promise y'all that

To my haters and all the people that counted me out I wish y'all the BEST

To my Readers all I want to say to you is next time you hear someone say they a Real Nigga just keep in mind "Loyalty Is Thin" and the definition of real now means

REMEMBER
EVERYBODY
AINT
LOYAL

and my reader behind the G-wall because you locked up don't mean you can't do something useful to help your family

Financially ideas make millions

also go check out my bruh Gumbs Books

Thank you …King so Hat

CHAPTER 1

Location: Irvington Park, Irvington N.J

This meeting is now over AJ stated to the 80 or more thunder point homies at the meeting as all the homies walk up to pay their mandatory 40 dollars which they pay every week AJ lil brother Krazy J spots a black unmarked Crown Vic slow rolling past the park five' 0 five 0 krazy announce now everyone is ready to take flight this is now the third time this month the pigs raid one of their supposedly top secret meetings as AJ looks to the front exit of the park two more police car's are pulling up gang unit someone yells it's on now everyone takes off running like they are in a marathon hoping not to get caught up some homies even take it as far as dropping guns and drugs trying their best not to get caught with nothing AJ his right hand mans BH and Krazy J makes it to his car the triple black 2017 BMW 760li the three hop srt-8 in with AJ behind the wheel and the car comes to life in seconds and pulls out it's parking spot faster the it was started damn AJ yells out loud this is now the third this month a meeting got ran down on some body telling it's no way in hell not back to back like this big bro slow down Krazy J tells AJ shxt like this happens sometimes nobody not telling not under our hood AJ shakes his head the foolish things that comes out his lil brother mouth sometimes he can't understand how they are even brothers and if a pussy boy is telling under our hood I'm a kill'em Krazy J states as he pulls out his silver 40cal pistol, AJ changes the subject as he brings the black machine to the red light on Grove st BH count that money that you got from the meeting I know you couldn't of got much from the homies due to the pigs running down so on Sunday im a need you to go through all our blocks that's (tp) and collect that bread from everybody big bro real short and he'll be home by these next two months and I'm tryna have a nice bag and some wheels for him I don't understand why you giving him anything we the ones who did all the work to get the hood up Krazy J blurts out Krazy J I'm getting tired of ya bullshxt big bro made the way without him we wouldn't have no hood now fall back with ya bull shit and when he do touch show some respect to him I don't want it to be no falling outs between us ite? Whatever big bro yo it AJ it's only 1,500 right here I got ight cool put it in the glove box we bout to shoot to the block to see who made it out that park and see who got lock up so we could have them out by tonight as the black machine pulls up on the block 20th ave and 22nd st all you see out their are young and old people ages starting from 13 teen to 50yrs old this block is what a few call "homebase" because outta every block that's apart of their organization this is the block that shows the most love to each and every member no matter their dislikes it's also called home-base because this is where AJ, BH and Krazy J are from the same as the old man AJ parks the black machine on the block and he quickly notice the block money that's being made from the burgundy house ever scent AJ connect bought that new smack through homebase been doing number's as AJ BH and Krazy J jump out the car they are approach by their shot caller Bear, what's moving homie's? Bear states and he goes into their set handshake which show's their are united as one, with each one of the three man Bear what's it looking like so far? AJ question him big bro as you can see we back we ran outta smack four times already but ya mans Tommy came through as soon as I place the call to him, as he should AJ replies back as they walk to the spot which they call the house which belongs to a old crackhead chick by name of bad Tina bad Tina got her name from way back in the day when everybody thought she was the baddest female to walk the street's now she looks just like any old crackhead, burn out skinny and bumps all over her face but AJ, BH and Krazy J got mad love for bad Tina because she was their first sex partner and anytime they needed to lay low or was in need of a spot to take a jump off to bad Tina kept her house door open to all three of them as the four man stood on the porch, Krazy J took a newport box out from his pants pocket and lit up a new-port the cancer stick lit up like it was dip in gas Krazy J waved the new-port until the flame went out bro what the fuck I tell you about smoking that wet? AJ question Krazy J you know that's a no-no throw that shit away AJ you always thinking you somebody father Krazy J replied back I'm good matter a fact I'm going up the block to the store I'll get up with y'all tomorrow if I make it past the night us! Krazy J walks off with AJ eyes burning holes into his back bro let him be we in our hood just let it go he'll be ite BH tells AJ and how the fuck do you know that AJ asks BH yeah we in our hood but bullets could come flying any second, he keep testing me he gonna be outta the set AJ you know ya lil brother hard headed but he's no fool when it's comes to the street's BH replies back yeah bro right Bear states, Bear don't you have a block to oversee AJ you right AJ I'm gone, BH I just don't want nothing to happen to him you know my moms already tripping out over us running the streets and if something happen to either one of us it'll kill her I feel you AJ but don't trip once the old man comes home you could fall back and let him run the set I hope so BH I hope so

AJ

We made a bond to the very end I got my homie and my best friend no-matter what no-matter what as the future ringtone goes off AJ eyes open up and he grabs his phone hello? where the fuck you at AJ? the female ask over the other end of the phone who this? AJ replies back as he sits up on the cheap couch and it all comes to him where he's at in bad Tina living room oh so now it's who this let me remind you ya so call wife Kim, what you forgot my voice or you laid up with one of ya thot bitches? nah bay I'm at bad Tina house as soon as them word's left his mouth he regretted them what? oh so now you fucking crackheads? AJ it's three fifty am give me one reason why I shouldn't throw all ya shit out front because I really fell asleep and told BH to wake me up if I over slept so what happen then AJ? I don't know but it's been a long night I'm on my way home now well if the sun beats you home you mind as well don't even walk through them doors click, the phone call ends damn AJ thinks as he sits back he truly didn't have plans on over sleeping, as he stands up to get himself together AJ wonders where BH was at as he walks towards the back of the house where bad Tina bed-room is located at he kicks all the trash to the side that's in the walkway when he reaches bad Tina room he cracks the door open and looks inside their bad Tina and BH lay in bed both of them ass naked AJ shakes his head and closes the door back and makes his way to the front of the house AJ lets himself out the house locking the door behind him the block is now dead all that's around now are stray cat's and dog's as AJ walks to the black machine a black tinted loose Audi S4 pulls alongside of him the driver window rolls down and goes straight for his 357 that's on the right side of his waist AJ what's moving fool? d-shouts out from the car who that AJ quickly replies back still holding on tight to his cannon AJ is no fool just because they know his name don't mean these are any of his homies or friends inside the Audi D-low fool now AJ is fully aware of who is inside of the car but that don't stop him from slowing his walk to his car and the Audi keeps it's speed to a rolling pace right along side of AJ what's good bro? AJ replies back tryna see the reason behind D-low wiping up on him nothing much just riding thru for the most part but what you doing out so early AJ this ain't like you and you don't got none of ya shooters with you, you slipping first off D-low I'm my own man and I hold my own and second I'm a grown ass man and could be in my street's any-day or any-time ya street's D-low questions yeah my street's AJ shoots right back the black machine lights up from AJ hitting the unlock button, D-low eye's moves straight from AJ to the black machine I see you change up ya whip bra nah AJ replies back that's a rental, yeah ok but AJ watch ya self out here they saying this block what y'all call it home-base? doing number's and you know how people could start hating and wanna get you out the way cuz you making money, I'm a keep that in mind D-low ite bro the Audi takes off doing what they are known to do take off as AJ starts the black machine his mind play's back the conversation he just had with D-low the block doing number's now and haters I gotta call a meeting for the block asap AJ tell himself because he knows when money start coming in so does the hate.

20 MINUTES LATER AJ

Exting the garden state parkway in Paterson N.J AJ checks his mirror's to make sure he wasn't followed home because this day and age you can't trust not a soul it's not like the old era their is no more honor, trust or loyalty amongst no one and these young kids killing people just to be down, as AJ goes around his block east 22nd st one more time he notice him and his wife Kim bed-room light is still on, damn I thought she'll be back to sleep by now, as AJ pulls into his backyard and parks his car along side of his wife white 2017 bmw x6, he knows he in for a long night, AJ exit his car and walks to the back door once he unlock the door he steps inside quickly closing the door and then walking to the a,t,d alarm box pad to reset the alarm, once done with that he walks to the closet and puts his 357 in the lock box takes off his shoes because Kim hates for him or anyone else for that matter to walk around the house with their shoes on, AJ makes his way thru the house to the stairs which leads him to the second floor of the house where his and Kim bed-room is at and also their son lil AJ room is at, AJ first walks to his son room and cracks the door open, lil AJ lays in bed with his batman night light on, AJ closest the door back and walks to the room he shares with Kim, AJ opens the door and Kim is sitting up in bed with the tv on love and hip hop AJ hates the show but Kim loves it Kim goes right in on AJ before he could even speak a word to her, so now you sleeping over crackhead house's while me and our son are here not knowing where you are at or even if you are alive, I'm telling you AJ I'm tired of this life you living it was fun when we were young but now it's time for you to get it together, ite Kim don't fucking ite Kim me I'm tried AJ and if something happens to you what are me and lil AJ gonna do? nothing is gonna happen to me Kim, and how the fuck do you know that? AJ you know what I'm done with this conversation if you don't care neither do I Kim I got you just give me a few months I'll be able to chill and fall back right now right now what AJ? what that gang needs you, you really need to open ya eyes AJ the street's are over their is no more loyalty, loyalty is a thing of the past and if you ever pull some shit how you did tonight and be laid up with some crackhead bitch again you gonna be finding you a new family, and go wash ya ass you not bout to be getting into my bed smelling like anything that ever died ite Kim you got it, I know I got it Kim states and turns over to go to sleep what a night AJ tells himself as he get ready to take a shower.

10 MINS LATER

AJ stands in the shower with the water running over his body he starts to reminisce about him and Kim, AJ met Kim at Irvington high school they both shared the same gym class AJ was always with the in crew but for Kim she always stay to herself she never tried to be down or act like no one she wasn't and you never caught difference dudes up in her face, AJ and Kim started going out as a couple after AJ stop the gcg girl's from jumping Kim on her way home from school, the gcg girls was just hating on Kim because she stay to herself and she plus she was pretty 5'6 light skin big booty and had a smile that'll make your grandfather wish he was still young from that day on AJ and Kim were always together they ate lunch together an walk to and from school together, Kim mother Ms.Pat loves AJ like he was her own son, Kim father Joe that was another story he hated everything about AJ but the feelings were mutual because AJ dislike him to but after some time Kim father learn how much AJ loved his baby girl and how much she loved him back so it was either get with the program or else AJ moms V-nasty fell in love with Kim the first time AJ brought Kim to the house, V-nasty knew Kim was the one for AJ and she didn't miss a day to remind him that AJ brother's and sister's also love Kim AJ smiled when he thought about his mom and Kim relationship as the saying goes your momma knows best.

CHAPTER 2

AJ, Kim & LIL AJ

Daddy daddy AJ son lil AJ yells and run into the bedroom and jumps on the bed daddy me and mommy was waiting up for you last night what time you got home daddy? boy stop playing with me before I jab you, no you not I'm a big boy daddy I could fight, yeah let me see lil AJ throw to slow punches at his father ok that's enough go get ready ok mommy lil AJ runs off to get ready where y'all going AJ question Kim? Kim shoots AJ a dirty look do it matter mr I sleep over crackhead houses now Kim I told you I ain't mean to, we going to breakfast with my mother and father Kim tells AJ cutting him off from saying whatever he was about to say why you coming with us? Kim ask real smart nah AJ replies back I got some things to handle today yeah whateva lil AJ hurry up before I hurt ya father, ok mommy lil AJ yells back AJ at least you could go check on the daycare see if them crackheads you hired finish fixing the floors mommy I'm ready lil AJ tells his mother as he walks into AJ and Kim bed-room ite give ya father a kiss and let's go lil AJ hugs and kiss his father love you daddy love you to and tell your grandma and grandpa I sent my love to them ok lil AJ tells his father.

3 HOURS LATER

After a shower and getting dress AJ is back ready to hit the streets again yo-gotti I'm sorry ringtone comes on AJ phone yoo whats good my boy? Vickie what's good? nothing much where you at AJ?

on my way to the hood why what's good? nothing just wanted to see you that's all nah I can't do nothing today oh wifey got you on lock-down? nah I got a lot of running around to do today what-eva nigga just hit a bitch up when you free click, damn moe drama AJ thinks he should never had started fucking with this jump bitch Vickie but the story's he heard about her he had to see if they were true it was true she had some good pussy but no one ever told him she'll be acting like this all crazy and shit as AJ jumps on the parkway heading south toward Newark plies ringtone comes on 15yrs damn pussy ass people gave my nigga 100 years had is momma leaving out the courtroom in tears hello you have a prepaid call from inmate da don to refuse this call hang up to accept this call dial one to hello? what's good bro? nothing much just on my way to the hood yeah yo good looking with that bread last week but I told you I ain't need it I got like 3 days left to max out oh you counting down now? what happen to all that do ya time don't let ya time do you talk? yo AJ you a funny dude nah doe bro let the homies in their use it I know they need it, I was already gonna do that the old man tells AJ but on the real AJ I got a lot of plan's put together for us, we going str-8 to the top I'm a need you with me, I'm back in tune with the homies from south Central la, bro I already told you I'm falling back once you touch AJ tells the old man cutting him off, come on AJ we back to this again? year bro it's same I got a family now and all things has changed from the 10yrs you been gone, AJ what you saying AJ everybody got a family, yeah you right but I'm tryna be on the street's with mines, AJ I keep telling you you not gonna have to do nothing, you in power already and once you stop playing and step up and take this triple og you really not gonna have to do nothing look bro AJ states really upset now because not only is the old man tryna force status on AJ but he talking reckless over a jailhouse phone call which is a no-no, bro I'm a talk to you, about it once you home face to face I'm on the parkway and you know how them state boyz boyz hate to see a young black male shining and driving something better then they got, what kind a whip you got now the old man ask? 2017 bmw 760li AJ tells him and check his mirror's for the police, word up I just saw one of those in the car book the lil homie got, what color? black you already know the shit, yeah that's the color I would had got well it's yours AJ tells him, yeah ite you playin lil bro it's your big bro AJ tells him, well hold my bitch down for me but for the most part I love you lil bro, I love you more bro us click AJ ends the call now all I gotta do is hit Tommy cousin Big-dawg up and see what kind of new wheel's he got at his car lot AJ tells himself.

MEANWHILE ON THE SOUTH-SIDE OF NEWARK N.J, NA-JAY & FAT-KAT

Na-jay I'm telling you I caught the dude AJ lacking last night D-low tells him, Na-jay just stands there with all different types of reasoning running through his mind of why AJ was out on his block 4 in the morning, D-low you ain't see him with no bag or nothing? Na-jay questions him, nah bro but his hand stay on his right side hip, I know he was holding a gun their but I ain't see it, and you say he was driving a new 760 bmw?, yeah bro all black shit looked mean is hell, ite look when you come back through I got something for you, Na-jay tells him, na you ain't gotta pay me pay me I just wanna be apart of the family, and I'm telling you all this to show you my loyalty, ite let me run it pass all the bro'z and if they agree we'll bring you in, Na-jay tells him but he's lying, D-low will never be apart of Na-jay movement D-low is what you call a man-hoe he always running around town tryna get down with ant crew that's doing anything, D-low is not to be trusted he'll do anything to be apart of something and anything for some money, ite na I'll swing back through this week, ite bro you do that Na-jay tells him as D-low pulls off Na-jay is approach by his shot-caller Black, and his right hand mans Fat-kat, what that fool want? Fat-kat asks Na-jay he claim he saw AJ leaving his block home-base at 4am yesterday, word he might of been dropping that work off around that time and word on the street's they got the best smack in town right now Black tells both of his big bro'z, yeah so I heard Na-jay says getting real heated look Black this is what I want you to do Fat-kat tells him taken over the conversation put a four man team together and have them ride them fools block and watch they movement and more then that, so we could know if that's what's going on AJ dropping that work off at that time, tell who-eva you pick to report every-thing them fools do to you Black I need you on this right now, ite big bro I'm on it right now Black tells Fat-kat and steps off to go handle the call Na-jay what's good bro why you look so upset? Kat man I hate that dude AJ and every-time his name comes up I just wanna murder his ass, bro his time gonna come and when it does we'll kill him and any body with him but for now we gotta shoot to Paterson to have this meeting with our top people, you right Kat let's roll out.

LOCATION ROBBERY AND HOMICIDE, BANGER, DET. KILLBURG & DET. JACKSON

Wake up ass hole Det.Killburg tells Banger as he and his partner Det.Jackson walks into the interview room, damn man y'all had me in this cold ass room all night Banger tells both of the Det.'s, if it was up to me you'll be in a worse place than this, Det.Killburg tells him but my partner wants to save ya black ass, for whatever reason I don't know, look Rome, Banger or what-eva you wanna go by we not getting nowhere with running down at them meetings for one we ain't catch nobody we found gun's and drugs which is alright but we don't have no one to place with it what we need from you Det. Jackson tells him is for you to wear a wirer or a camera to one of them meeting's or for you to tell us where ya organization put their guns and drugs at? help us help you Banger, Det.Killburg tells him, these guys don't care about you or ya family if you go to jail they not gonna be there to help you or your family out we the ones help you me and my partner so what's it's gonna be Det.Jackson question him ite I'll do it which one Det.Killburg ask him ready to wirer or camera Banger up I'll wear the camera Banger tells them, and puts down his head, Banger you are a smart man Det.Jackson tells him we'll have you up and ready to go in another hour Det.Jackson tells him while he and his partner make their way out the interview room damn Banger thinks to himself how did I get myself into all this snitching shit the homies gonna murder me if they find out!

CHAPTER 3

Banger 6 month's earlier

B anger you dirty dick nigga you burn me Missy tells Banger over the other end of the phone, come get ya shit outta my house before I throw all this shit out, what bitch I ain't burn you you must of got burn by one of them other nigga's you fucking, other nigga's you the only fuck boy I been dealing with, you know what just come get ya shit Banger I'm not playing ite I'm on my way, this bitch trippin Banger tells himself I couldn't of burn her my shit don't hurt when I piss, Banger speeds through block's trying his hardest to make it to Missy house on South Orange ave and 8ᵗʰ st before she through all his shit out, which he knows she's good for what Banger don't know is it's a unmark following his g37, as Banger pulls up in front of Missy house the unmark slow rolls pass and parks down the block, Banger jumps out his car, without paying any mind to the unmark and goes straight to Missy front door which is unlock as Banger steps inside one of his shoes coming flying pass his head, yo what the fuck Banger shouts out, nigga get ya shit and go that's what da fuck Missy replies back Missy stop playing games you know I couldn't of burn you, so what you calling me a hoe? nah but nah but nothing grab shit and go you know what cool and don't call me telling me to come home, nigga I'm done with you Missy tells Banger after 10 minutes of packing his stuff Banger makes his exit fuck Missy and their 5 year relationship, I got hoes for days after putting everything in his car Banger pulls off heading toward central ave to his jump off chick tt house on north Munn in East Orange N.J Banger stops at the light on 8th st and Central ave he looks in his mirror and notice a unmarked police car right behind him damn I hope that's not the pigs in that car and just some call hood nigga's that wanna look like the policeBanger can't understand why so call thug's wanted to look like the police as the light change Banger heart is starting to race with him taken all his stuff outta Missy house which was his drugs, choppa and money and also his outfit's Banger is hoping that they don't pull him over he doesn't have any licenses and he been smoking weed all day inside the car so he knows it smell like weed in the car Banger makes a left turn forgetting to use his signal the dumbest mistake he could have eva done the unmark active it's lights to pull him over, thoughts run through Banger mind to take chase but he knows for one he doesn't have the wheel to take chase, so he does somewhat of the right thing and pulls over the unmark pulls right behind him the two Det.'s Killburg and Jackson knew full well of who Banger was is, that's why they been following him all morning, they radio in for backup and step out the car and approach, the white g37 Det.Killburg walk to the driver side with his partner Det.Jackson taken the passenger side, both with their hands on their guns licenses and registration, Det.Killburg tells Banger while looking inside the car officer I don't have licenses but I have the registration Banger tells him well ass hole you shouldn't be driving now step out the car for what? Banger ask because I said so or you want me to drag you out, this some bull shit Banger states slowly getting out the car, put your hands behind your back, what I do? I said put ya fucking hands behind ya back after handcuffing Banger and placing him in the unmark car Det.Killburg and Det.Jackson back up showed up and they started to search Banger car within 5 mins they find everything and all Banger could think about is the prison time he gonna get for all the stuff they found in his car, once the tow truck comes and takes away Banger car, the two Det.'s get back inside the unmark with Banger in the back seat so kid this can go one or two ways Det.Jackson tells Banger, we know who you are and what gang you apart of, but we don't really want you we want the top dawg AJ now if you could help us we could help you and everything we found today could all go away, you got time to think about it we'll be at the station, in less than 10 mins, Banger already had his mind made up he ain't even need the 10 mins they gave him, once Det.Jackson offer that deal it was AJ that was going down not Banger.

V- NASTY HOUSE

knock, knock, knock, who the hell knocking on my door like they the police ma it's me Qyanazia tells her mother V-nasty from the other side of the door me who? Qyanazia ma open the door what the hell you want? V-nasty question her daughter I still do live here well where are your keys if you live here, I lost them the other day, girl you lose so much stuff I won't be surprised if you lost ya self and where you coming from eight in the morning, ma stop playing and let me in V-nasty opens the door and let her daughter inside the house, and where were you last night miss fast ass? ma I'm grown now you know what? oh you grown but you still living in my house girl bye V-nasty tells her and steps off to go back to watch tv as Qyanazia makes her way to her bedroom she hears the music coming out her lil brother Bar-man room she shakes her head because all he play's is jay-z like he's some type of old head but he's only 19 teen him and his twin sister Qwae-ma after making it to her room and closing the door Qyanazia then start's to get undress she had a long night of partying with her new guy friend buzz, Qyanazia is really feeling buzz, she just hope the feeling's are the same

ma who was that? Qwae-ma asks stepping into the living-room that wasn't nobody but ya fast ass sister coming in here at some damn 8am that girl needs to slow down because I ain't bout to be watching nobody damn babies I know that's right ma me either but ma I need a few dollars so I could check these book's out the library I want girl if you don't get outta my face with that you need money for some books at the library go ask ya stepfather Kintahe I ain't got no more money shit I'm waiting for ya brother to bring me some money now, which one? Qwae-ma question her mother which one you think you know damn well Krazy J don't got no-money, AJ now that's who you need to ask for some money when he gets here when-eva that is, ite ma but for now I'm a go ask Kintahe where he at anyway, he in that damn garage, after walking to the garage Qwae-ma spot's her step-father fixing on his car, hey you what brings you in here? I need some money so I could get some books from the library, how much you need? 25-dollars that's it? Kintahe says and goes into his pocket and pulls out a 50-dollar bill, keep the rest for yourself, and Qwae-ma yes? stay into them book's we all counting on you to make it life, I know step dad she tells him, ite go head to the library and get ya learn on, love you baby girl, love you to Qwae-ma replies back.

MEANWHILE IN PATERSON N.J KIM

Kim sits with her son lil AJ her dad and mom at a breakfast spot, Kim what's on your mind why you look so down, her mother questions her nothing ma it's ok I'm just not hungry, Kim this your mother talking to you, I carried you for 9 months I know when something not right with you, baby girl are you feeling well Kim father Joe jumps into the conversation, yeah dad I'm good is it that boy AJ because you know I'll jump on his ass, Joe tells Kim no dad Kim laughs, Kim finds it funny but she also knows Joe would really try to fight AJ lil AJ you almost done eating? yes well hurry up Kim how about you let me and ya dad take lil AJ for the weekend you go home and get some rest you sure ma? yeah and I think lil AJ would like that, lil AJ you wanna go home with me and grandpa? lil AJ nod's his head up and down, ite I love y'all Kim stands to leave giving each person a kiss at the table before making her exit.

NA-JAY & FAT-KAT

Bro why did you agree on meeting the bro'z at this breakfast spot all the way in Paterson? Na-jay question Fat-kat because they wanted to have a sit down and what better way to handle a boss meeting with food on the table? kat you a funny dude Na-jay tells Fat-kat cracking up laughing, where the parking-lot? right here damn bro you see that bad bitch that just step out the breakfast spot? where? Fat-kat asks taking his attention off finding a parking spot to look at the female, that's walking to a white bmw x6 oh shit na that's AJ wife right there you talking bout you lying Na-jay tells him, how you know? you forgot I went to Irvington high school with AJ, AJ and her on some high school sweetheart shit. Yeah well pull up on her I'm bout to send that bitch nigga a message, nah nah chill how about we follow the bitch and where they live or learn her routine, we could kill two birds with one stone, find the money and work and kill AJ kat that's why I love you so much because you a smart is hell so hurry up and bust a u-turn an follow this bitch we just gotta set up another meeting with the bro'z that won't be about nothing I'm a call them while we follow her Fat-kat tells Na-jay.

CHAPTER 4

Rain & Krazy J

S hoot the dice why you holding on to them so long Rain tells Krazy J bitch I'll shoot the dice when I feel like it, Krazy J I'm not bout to be to many more bitches what you gonna do? you could always get a fair one Krazy J tells Rain, bitch you gang bangin like everyone else fuck you talking about? ite Krazy J keep testing me, what-eva dawg Krazy J shoot's the dice and ace's out pay me my money Rain tells Krazy J, Krazy J is hot they been shooting dice now for an hour and Krazy J just lost the lost 50 dollars he had bitch I'm not paying you shit bitch, as soon as that word came out Krazy J mouth Rain had her burgundy handle 44 long out, and in Krazy J face, bro I told you I was not bout to be 2 many more of ya bitches, now where my cash at Krazy J or do you wanna be laid you in UMD,N.J, ha, ha ha Rain you funny is hell Krazy J, tells her you not shooting nothing, now get this big ass gun out my face, because you turning me on with this gangster shit you doing, and I know you love girl's so stop playing before you be loving me yo what the fuck y'all doing AJ yells through the driver window of the black machine nothing bro I'm just tryna teach Rain that having fear aint for man, Krazy J tells AJ Rain what's going on? AJ asks her ya krazy ass brother won't pay me my money, what he gotta give you money for? we were shooting dice, hold on y'all were gambling y'all know that's against the rule's, Rain put that gun up and go hold the block down, but bro he gotta give me my money, take it as a lost, y'all wasn't supposed to be gambling anyway, Rain

16

stomps off mad and Krazy J stands their smiling, Krazy J get in the car AJ orders him Krazy J takes his cool old time getting into the car what's good bro? nothing AJ replies back pulling off as soon as Krazy J gets in the car, Krazy J you been tripping lately what's good with that? nah bro I was just having fun, yeah with a gun in your face, Rain ain't killing no body AJ only thing she killing is the pussy she be eating, Krazy J look this how we bout to do this, I need you with me 24 hours I need you to be my eye's, AJ I love you and all bro but I ain't tryna be with you all day long, I got shit I gotta do to and what's that? AJ question his brother, man I just got shit I gotta do whateva j, as the brothers roll through the city in the black machine, AJ gets a call from his connect Tommy, Tommy what's good bro? AJ I need to see you asap, ight I could be to you in 15 mins, ight I'm at the house in Maplewood I'm their click j put ya seat belt on we bout to shoot to go see Tommy at his spot in Maplewood, and I don't need them pig's pulling us over for no reason, fuck them pig's bro you worried about them pulling us over we got a army to, Krazy J just put ya seat-belt on, ight big bruh.

12MIN'S LATER

AJ and Krazy J pulls up in front of the connect Tommy house come on bro AJ tells Krazy J, after they parked the car, as they make their way to the front door they are greeted by Tommy lil sister Ashley, hey y'all Ashley says to the two brother's, nothing much AJ replies back, where ya brother at? he in the back yard y'all know the way, hey Ashley Krazy J says hey Krazy Ashley how old are you now, I'm 23 Krazy why? oh nothing, I'll see you around Krazy J tells her and give her a look like he wanted to sex her right their in the front of the house j come on AJ tells him and leave that girl alone she don't want you, AJ you always hatin, I know she wants me by the way she looks at me, nah the way she looks at you should tell you she truly thinks you are crazy as the brothers make their way through the million dollar house passing all kinds of artwork on the wall's and family picture's, the brothers get to the back glass door and exit the house, Tommy and two other guy's stand their watching two pit-bulls fight Tommy what's good? AJ asks Tommy o' AJ what's good youngin? bucky break that fight up we'll finish another time, ight Tommy one of the guys replies back to him, AJ, Krazy J step over here to the garage with me close the door Krazy J Tommy tells him after taken his seat at the round table with AJ so Tommy what's good? AJ ask ready to get to the reason he here, look AJ you know I got some people on the inside in high places and I got a call and ya name came up on the watch list for the police, I don't know what you doing or what's going on, but AJ I can't become hot because of you my family needs me ant the money I make and I can't make money if I'm lock up or being watch, get what I'm saying? nah I don't get what you saying AJ tells Tommy getting real upset, what you saying Tommy you bout to stop selling to us? AJ listen to me I'm not saying that but what I'm saying is you need to check ya organization because someone is telling what you saying? Krazy J ask you disrespecting my set we ain't no rat's dawg Krazy J chill out AJ tells him, AJ we gonna have to chill out until we find out who's telling on you let me push up on my people's and once I get news about it I'll let you know who the person is or who the people are Krazy J gives Tommy a look that makes him lower his eye's I'll get that to you AJ then we could start back moving out ight what-eva AJ tells Tommy real heated standing up to make his exit AJ grab that bag right there by the door that's 3,000 brick's of dope that should hold you over until I get word from my people, ight cool the two brother's dap Tommy up and exit the garage, they make their way back threw the house and Krazy J looks around and then knock a family picture off the wall, why you do that for j AJ ask his brother man fuck that nigga he tryna say some body telling under our hood, Krazy J replies back and makes his exit out the house, only my brother AJ says to himself as he walks behind his brother out the front door.

BH

Damn that feels so good you like that daddy yeah keep going BH lays back on the stink smelling bed which belongs to none other then bad Tina, bad Tina is giving BH the best blow-job he ever had in his life, bad Tina sucks BH off to the best of her ability hoping to get some more crack they been smoking all last night, o'o' right their BH tells her right before he busts all in bad Tina mouth damn Tina it feels better every-time, I know you my baby and it's my job to always make it better than the last time BH goes into his pocket and takes out 20 dollars worth of crack, this for you BH hands bad Tina the crack, you don't want none? nah I'm bout to hit the block BH says while pulling up his pants alright be safe out their bad Tina tells him while she starts to look for her tool's so she could smoke the crack, BH makes his way to the front door and lets himself out the house it's now three o'clock in the afternoon and the block is jumping as BH checks his surroundings, he steps off the porch and heads to the store up the block, BH wait up Bear yells to BH while coming across the street, big bro we need some more work at the burgundy house, what y'all need some d'boy or girl? nah big bro we good on the crack we need some more dope I been calling AJ man's phone all day and he ain't hit me back that's not like him, did you call AJ yet? yeah I called him to but he ain't answer either, ight give it about another hour if they don't hit you back, I'm a call one of the bro's to bring a few brick's through just to keep the money moving BH tells Bear big bro you see that car coming down the block? Bear says yeah what it? BH asks well that's their second time coming thru here the Gray Audi S4 rides past BH and Bear and makes a right turn on 20th ave and 22nd st heading toward 19th ave big bro what's good? Rain asks BH as she approach him and do their set handshake nothing much Rain how you been? I been doing alright bro but I had to whip out the cannon out on Krazy J ass over a dice game, why what happen? BH asks her yo big bro their go that car again, what car ask Rain, just before the car whip up on the three, guns blasting boc, boc, boc, boc boom boom boom boom, all three take off running but Rain wasn't so lucky she attempted to reach for her 44 long, but that was the dumbest thing she could done, two shots take her face off, she died before she hit the ground, for BH and Bear they cut through the alley on the side of the building running for their life bullet's flying pass them, damn near taken off their heads boom boom boom Bear and BH cut left behind the alley and hop the gate which brings them on 21ˢᵗ they both are out of air, damn Bear who could that have been? BH question him I don't know bro but I know when I looked back Rain was laid out on the ground Bear tells BH damn come on Bear I hear sirens, lets get outta here.

CHAPTER 5

Na-jay & Fat-kat

S low up kat she bout to turn in the driveway right there how you know Fat-kat asks Na-jay fool she got her turn signal on just keep riding pass her, she pulling into the blue house driveway, unbeknown to Kim Fat-kat and Na-jay been following her for the past 15 minutes she been driving to her house from having breakfast with her mother and father, Kim thoughts been so much on AJ that she wasn't paying any attention to her mirror's and AJ been school Kim on that number one rule, because he knows that dudes would love to run up in his house, so kat you think you we should take the chance now and run up in his spot? Na-jay asks nah bro Fat-kat tells him, why not? Na-jay replies back with his face all twisted up, because how about she don't even know where the safe at? and not for nothing it's daylight out right now how would it look my fat ass with a face-mask on knocking on some body door with this neighborhood, I know somebody gonna see us, Fat-kat tells Na-jay, kat that's why I fucks with you, you smart is hell I wish I had two of you Na-jay tells Fat-kat, but you know how to get back to the hood from here right? questions Fat-kat yeah it's easy let just do our homework then we gonna run up in the spot while that pussy boy there, an kill him and take all the money and drugs up in their, Fat-kat tells Na-jay, ight let's get up outta here then, before somebody sees us, you think we could still meet up with the homie's before we go back to Newark? because the next time I come out here I'm tryna run up in AJ bitch ass houseNa-jay tells Fat-kat

21

ight I'm a hit them up now, Fat-kat replies back the relationship these two share is crazy, they both grew up in the same hood, and been running together scent they were 10yrs old, but Fat-kat always been the brains, when the gang life hit the streets of Newark, Fat-kat wasn't off it but Na-jay being the loose one he join up asap later on down the line Na-jay brought Fat-kat in Fat-kat being the smart one he saw a opportunity to make money, he saw how everyone respected Na-jay because of his status, and they did everything he told them to do weather dumb shit or not so Fat-kat join and from then on he control every situation from the back letting Na-jay be the leader, with Na-jay power an Fat-kat smarts they been able to control their set an make a lot of money.

KIM

After parking her truck in the backyard and going in the house, Kim is tried from stressing over AJ and being up till 4am last night, Kim just wants to take a hot bath and go to bed with her, parents taken lil AJ home with them Kim is so thankful for that with AJ running the streets all day Kim always has lil AJ 24 hours a day here we go here we go again now you telling me she's just a friend, trina ringtone goes off letting Kim know she has a in coming call, hello? is this Kim? a female voice asks over the other end of the phone it all depends on who? wants to know Kim replies back, this phone call doesn't feel right to Kim, well this is Vickie the female over the other end says and Kim cuts her right off I don't know any Vickie and how you get my number? Kim says that's neither here nor there how I got your number but I was just calling to ask you what time you were gonna be done with our man because a bitch hot and ready an I need our man to come help me outta this situation he with you right? from the stress over AJ and being tried Kim goes all the way off on Vickie look you lil thot bitch I don't know what kind of games you playing or what but you got the right one this time when I catch your lil ass I'm a beat the brakes off that ass Kim tells Vickie well whatever Vickie responds back but from the way you coming I take it as our man not with you either, but tell bay last night was mad real, unknown to

Vickie AJ came home late last night from bad Tina house, bye bye click the phone call ends, Kim is now burning up inside she looks at the phone and speed dials AJ phone number, after two unsuccessful attempts of calling AJ phone Kim calls the only person she trust besides her parents an AJ her best friend Toya hello? Toya answer the phone hello? Toya asks again Kim why are you crying? Kim talk to me why are you crying? look Kim where are you? home Kim tells her and goes right back to crying, ight I'm on my way girl Toya tells Kim click, Kim is hurting inside this ain't nothing new, females been playing on Kim phone scent her an AJ were kids, but what has Kim so emotional now is because she's a month pregnant and AJ don't even know he's about to be a father of two.

AJ & KRAZY J

You want war we ready we got guns plus machete's want beef no, as the music plays loud inside the car as AJ an Krazy J ride through north Newark on their way to the safe house in Belleville N.J AJ doesn't hear his phone ringing and he is so caught up in his thoughts about Tommy not giving them no more work, he wouldn't even cared to answer that's how much he was in his feelings at the moment, yo you saw T-dub on that corner Krazy J ask AJ lowering the music, nah AJ replies back still not fully focus on what's going on around him, didn't he run off with them 100 bricks we gave him, Krazy J asks his brother, yeah AJ tells Krazy J well let me knock his shit off we can't have no body just getting off on us like that, Krazy J tells AJ you wanna hit'em AJ ask not caring they are in his car I'm a park around the corner just hit him up and cut through one of the side of these house's we still got these 3,000 brick's on us AJ tells his lil brother, ight I got you big bruh, I'm about to make him wish he never ran off with that work Krazy J tells AJ once Krazy J was out the car and cut through the side of the green house they were park in front of, AJ sits his head back on the headrest and close his eyes, damn he exhales in his mind he ask himself, what am I gonna do now? just when the going was just getting good AJ phone vibrates in the cupholder as soon as he look down to get it, he hears bloca, bloca,

bloca, bloca, bloca, 5 shots goes off, but after a second he hears 3 other shots sound off boom, boom, boom but it sounded like it was from a different gun shit AJ yells reaching for his 357 so he could go help his lil brother with who-ever was shooting at his as AJ was opening the driver door, he sees his lil brother running from the side of the green house, Krazy J jumps straight in the passenger seat, go, bruh go, AJ takes off in the machine asap, damn lil bruh what happen? AJ ask Krazy J once they were two blocks away, bruh I had him but he saw me walking toward him and he started talking some poppy shit to some dude's and they started looking my way on some krazy shit and when I took the 40cal I tried to air his poppy ass out but some poppy's came out the poppy store and started busting some big shi, I know everybody think I'm krazy bruh, but I'm not shit I know the rest of them poppy's were strap so I got the fuck outta their but I think I hit him bruh word up Krazy J tells AJ it's ight lil bruh we'll get him, AJ replies back but it wasn't ight AJ knew in his heart every action comes with a reaction and this was just added to all the rest of the bull shit that was happening in his life

CHAPTER 6

Qwae ma

D amn it's already eight o'clock I gotta hurry up and get home Qwae-ma thinks to herself after logging off the internet from facebook which V-nasty doesn't approve of none of her kids having because that's another why people just be all up in ya business after saying bye to the librarian Qwae-ma is on her way home for the night, but before anything else could happen a black Audi s4 pulls along side of her damn you cute is hell Shorty could I talk to you for a minute, no I'm good and you might be to old for me anyway Qwae-ma replies back well what's age? nothing but a number who cares about age in 2016, the driver of the Audi says, well I do and so does my mother and father Qwae-ma tells him, but he still does not give up well they ain't gotta know if you don't tell them and you'll look real good driving my car the driver says, no I'll pass Qwae-ma tells him well look you lil bitch I was tryna be nice and respectful to you I might of even gave your lil ass a ride home now your dumb ass gotta keep on walking the driver replies back, who are you talking to Qwae-ma asks stopping her walk, you I was gonna make you my pyt but now you just drop down to being my lil jump-off the driver tells Qwae-ma, whoever you are I'm a make sure I tell my brother's about you Qwae-ma says well make sure you tell them the right name to they call me D-low bitch, D-low says while taken off in the Audi burning rubber, ok Mr. D-low with your mad ass I'm a tell my brothers as soon as I make it home! Qwae-ma says to herself, what D-low ain't know was Qwae-ma was

AJ and Krazy J baby sister and they loved her to death had he knew he would have never disrespected her like that, Qwae-ma is not in the street's but the way her friends girl's and boys talk about her brother's she knows they are bout that life.

BH & BEAR

Bang, bang, bang who is it? a lil girl asks front the other side of the house door, it's daddy BH tells her mommy it's daddy can I open the door please, girl move Judy tells her and snatch the door open and where the fuck you been Judy questions BH what? BH replies Bear come on, and who the fuck is this nigga you bringing all up in my house Judy asks as both man walk pass her into the house but neither man responds back, daddy BH daughter yells and run an jump into his arms daddy I miss you she tells BH, I miss you to lil momma, know he don't Ashey and don't be lying to my daughter Judy says to BH, Judy shut the fuck up BH tells her and walks into the living-room carrying his baby girl in his arms, with Bear one step behind, yo could you sit on the couch over their Bear, I'm bout to go take a shower, Judy take me out some thing to wear BH tells her as they step into the bed-room, what? hold on girl Judy tells her friend lady who's on the other end of the phone, nigga have you lost your mind you come in my house after being out all night with who knows, and expect me to just jump up and do all you say fool you trippin you better get your own shit out fuck wrong with you, Ashley you to your room BH tells his daughter placing her on the floor, ok daddy she replies once Ashley closes her bed-room door BH is across the room with both hands wrap around Judy neck, what the fuck I tell you about talking to me like that, you think I'm a game BH asks Judy while shaking her a lil by the neck, due to being just shot at BH is in war mode, and is ready to kill, Judy smart mouth just got caught up at a bad time BH I'm sorry Judy manage to get out, daddy your hurting mommy BH daughter tells him coming back into the room might have just saved Judy life, BH lets go of Judy neck and looks into her eye's the look in her eye's is a look of hurt and pain through all the times they had a fight this time was the closest BH ever came to killing Judy and she knows that BH grabs his traveling bag from under the bed and start throwing his clothes from the closet into the bag, while Judy holds their daughter and watch him like he was gonna turn around and kill her any minute baby girl I love you BH told his daughter while walking out the room, BH daughter doesn't even respond back, Bear let's roll BH tells Bear while making his way to the front door, I thought you were bout to wash up? Bear replies back getting up from where he was sitting, nah it's been a change of plan's let's go BH tells Bear again …

10:30 PM T-DUB

Everybody can I have your attention? thank you this meeting is now in so who ever talks outta turn they getting a dp let's let that beknown, the leader of the poppy's lu takes control of the meeting now earlier today we had someone come to our neighborhood and shoot at our brother t we all know that can't go without retaliation we going out tonight and kill anybody who had something to do with it, no one disrespect our block no one now I have a few questions for you t do you know this guy that came through here earlier? lu asks t, t is scared outta his mind t doesn't know if his brothers are upset over the situation or not some of them already didn't agree on him being apart of their brother-hood because he was a blood and they already know bloods do not accept no one leaving outta their nation, yeah I know who he is his name is Krazy J and his brother goes by AJ and from what Joey mother said about how the driver of the car that was in front of her house look, I know for a fact that was him who was driving the car t tells lu, so is their any other reason why they would want your head other then you were apart of (tp) lu asks t t thought long and hard about it he knew that if he told his brothers about the bricks of dope he beat the brothers for they would want in and t wasn't man enough to tell them no so he went out like the sucker he was and ain't keep it real, no that's the only reason I could think of t replied back, lu gave t a look that said he ain't believe him but being as he was a brother he had to take his word for it, taken back over the meeting lu tells everybody their to be on point because if what I hear of them (tp) guy's they deep and would go to war with the united states army if it came to it, so stay strap at all times and watch your brothers back this meeting is now over Lu tells everybody at the meeting, I'm my brothers keeper, I'm my brother keeper all the rest of the poppy's yells which brings the meeting to an end ...

CHAPTER 7

AJ & Krazy J

Bruh you sure you lock up the safe the right way? I don't need know mistakes AJ tells Krazy J as they get back into the car from putting up the drugs in their safe house in Belleville N.J, yeah bruh I'm not dumb Krazy J replies back, I never said you were dumb j I just, you know what nevermind where you want me to drop you off at? I'm about to take it on in the house I had enough for one day and don't have it in me for nothing else AJ tells Krazy J well just jump on the parkway I'm going to p-town with you we been together all day mind is well finish the day off together, I could get use to this you know? it ain't like I got any-body to go home to, I'll sleep in the guest room, I'm not really up to hearing mom-dukes and Kintahe talk about changing my life tonight Krazy J tells AJ ight that's what we gonna do I got stuff I never wore at the house an we the same size, s just give you something or you could pick it out AJ says that's why I love you big bruh Krazy J replies back ...

30 MINS LATER IN PATERSON, N.J

Big bruh every-time I come to your house which ain't alot but when I do I just wanna move in with y'all yo is my nephew here? Krazy J asks AJ he should be Kim truck here AJ replies back, oh ain't that Toya benz? Krazy J asks AJ yeah that's her car AJ says back baby I'm home Krazy J announce once both of the brother's enter the back door, the music was on in the living room so that's where both of the brothers went, what's good bay? what's good Toya AJ asks both the women who were both sitting on the couch eating pizza, hey Kim respond back hey AJ Toya said back damn AJ not the only one here Krazy J say to both women hey j Kim says j we see you Toya tells him while rolling her eye's, Toya an Krazy J have a love hate relationship, Krazy J was Toya first sex partner but after Krazy J hit it he stop answering Toya phone calls, after a while Toya gave up calling him and move on, well can I have some pizza? Krazy J ask it's a box in the oven Kim tells him AJ takes a long look at Kim and something is off with his wife she never greeted him with a hey, well Kim I'm out girl it's been real AJ take care of my girl good night to you to, Toya tells them both ight Toya good-night to you AJ tells her back, once Toya was gone out the room Kim spoke is Krazy J staying the night? yeah he gonna sleep in the guest room, an where is my son? AJ asks he with my mother an father if you would have answered your phone today you would have knew that Kim tells AJ you ain't call my phone my phone was in the cup holder all day that's where it's at now AJ tells Kim look AJ I'm tired I'm going to bed Kim says getting off the couch, but AJ stood in front of her blocking Kim from going anywhere what's wrong bae AJ asks Kim breaks down crying AJ I can't keep living like this one of your thot bitches call my phone today telling me when I'm done with you for the day to send you to her what one of my bitches I don't got no bitches AJ lies to Kim right in her face what she say her name is anyway? AJ asks she said her name Vickie Kim tells him Vickie? man I don't know any Vickie's AJ replies back well she sure is hell knows you an also knew you ain't come home last night so can you please explain that for me? Kim say bae I don't know what kind of games that whoever she is, is playing but I don't know her or how she knew about me making it home late last night you know them bitches out their wanna fuck up what we got AJ tries his best to change Kims thinking but the look in her eye's says she not believing nothing that AJ has said, look AJ I'm about to go up stairs to bed and tomorrow I'm a take a few things with me to my parents house and stay there for a while all this is to much right now, so you just gonna let somebody fuck up what we got? AJ asks not at all it's you that's letting people fuck up what we have so on that note can you please move to the side I'm tired and I think it's best that you sleep in the living room or in the guest room with your brother tonight, good-night AJ Kim says and walk pass him to their bedroom, damn big bruh what happened to Kim? she looked real sad when she just walk pass me Krazy J asks AJ Vickie called her phone today claiming that I'm also her man AJ tells Krazy J, Krazy J just shakes his head damn big bruh you fucking up I'll Vickie if you want me to Krazy J tells AJ, nah lil bruh I'm good AJ replies back, well you want some of this pizza this shit good is hell Krazy J says yeah I'll take some I haven't ate all day …

KRAZY J & AJ

Go tell'em it's a homicide murder murder so we riding so tell'em it's a homicide the future and snoop-dogg ringtone goes off, Krazy J answers his phone what's poppin? yo where y'all at bruh? BH ask over the other end of the phone I'm at AJ spot why what's good? Krazy J asks oh y'all together? BH replies back yeah why? Krazy J asks, because I been blowing up AJ phone all day an night yesterday and he never pick up and I just remembered he made your krazy ass buy a phone so I called your phone BH says, man he ain't make me do shit dawg Krazy J replies back, yeah whatever j but where AJ at? BH says he right here sleep Krazy J replies back, well wake him up this shit is important BH tells Krazy J what happen? Krazy J asks because if it was about killing he wanted in first, killing people wasn't about fame to Krazy J he just loved the rush he felt when he pop off his pistol or choppa, bruh Rain got killed yesterday and I been calling AJ phone but y'all at his place playing house and shit BH tells Krazy J, man nobody not playing house we were handling business like the bosses we are Krazy J replies back boss? J put AJ on the phone BH says aight bitch nigga hold on, bruh wake up AJ wake up Krazy J tells his brother yeah J I'm up what's up AJ asks sitting up on the other bed in the guest room, the phone Krazy J tells him who is it? AJ asks man it's BH bitch ass Krazy J says well what do he want? AJb asks you ask him yourself Krazy J replies back while throwing the iphone to AJ Krazy J could care less about Rain being killed in Krazy J book you were born to die so why cry about it, yeah what's good BH? AJ asks once the phone was to his ear, bruh shit got real yesterday somebody came through the block and started shooting and the home-girl Rain got killed shit real bruh I'm on the block now and the police still deep out here they got the block shut down like the shit happen today, BH tells AJ hold slow down BH Rain got killed and the police got the block shut down, so that means no money is being made AJ asks money being made nigga I just told you the home girl got killed and you worried about money being made AJ you tripping out BH says over the phone, bruh it's not that I don't care about the home girl rip to her but people die every day but money can't be made when the police is around AJ replies back man man, man you really losing it AJ BH says hold slow down BH you sound high first off, what you took some pills or something? AJ asks, bruh I ain't take shit BH lies to AJ BH and bad Tina been up smoking crack all night long being as the police got the hood on lock BH had one of the lil homies shut down the trap house and bring him his work, he didn't wanna risk the police getting a tip that it was a trap house on the block and raid it was a smart move at first first but once bad Tina started sexing BH she talk him outta a gram of crack first then got BH to hit the glass dick and once they started they never stop, well it sound like it to me AJ tells BH, bruh you bugging BH replies back I smoke a lil weed that's all BH says back, where you at? AJ question BH I'm at the (spot) BH replied back AJ just shakes his head he knows he gotta holla at BH about spending so much time with bad Tina because he knows how female's who smoke crack move, they'll try to turn you out just so they'll have a free get high all day, ight bruh sit tight I'm a hit you when me and lil bruh hit the city an you could meet us on 19th ave and 22nd st I'm not tryna have them pig's questioning me about nothing AJ says to BH ight cool bruh love you BH says back I love you more AJ replies back now AJ is sure BH is high off more then weed because the only time he talks that love you shit is when he's pill up or under the influence of whatever else he might have taken.

9:30 AM KIM

I shouldn't have left like that Kim tells herself as she drives her bmw jeep to her parent's house, I could have at least woke him up and told him I was leaving the house, as that thought comes into Kim mind another thought comes in and tells her he didn't deserve you to wake him up and tell him you were leaving out the house, he fuck up not you, to shut her thoughts up Kim turns the radio on and the song that plays is can't be without you by mjb a tear falls outta Kim right eye the song brings so much pain to her she would hate to be without AJ but right now she just need time away from him, Kim knows the girl Vickie ain't just call her phone to play games these side bitches nowadays always overstepping their place, Kim knows a nigga gonna be a nigga but don't let it hit home Kim is know fool to the streets but she also knows that all man don't cheat but when your man is in the street's it's only a matter of time before the streets come knocking on your house door …

CHAPTER 8

30mins later

K im parks her truck in front of her parents house and grabs her bags and makes her way to the front door, but before she could put her key in the lock the door opens, baby what are you doing here? Kim father Joe asks daddy I came to stay with y'all for a couple day's Kim replies back, Joe looks into his daughter eye's he knows something is not right Kim never came to the house to stay a couple days, once she moved out she never sleep at the house again, but Joe doesn't push on the situation he just steps to the side and let Kim into the house, just leave your bags I'll take them up to your room, go head to the kitchen that's where your moms and lil AJ is at they are making breakfast your right on time Joe tells Kim thanks daddy Kim tells him and drop's her bag's an make her way to the kitchen, Joe watch his baby girl walk away he knows something is up an he plans to call AJ and see what's going on because if someone hurts his only child he'll hurt them no matter who they are son-in-law or not, mommy lil AJ yells and runs to his mother as she walks into the kitchen hey baby Kim replies back to lil AJ an bends down to pick him up, grandma my mommy here, lil AJ tells Ms.Pat boy I'm old but I can see Ms.Pat tells her grandson, hey baby what brings you here? I thought you were coming to get him next sunday? Ms.Pat asks Kim no ma I'm not here to pick lil AJ up I'm here to stay a couple days, Kim replies back the look Ms.Pat gives Kim is a look of surprise, ma it's a long story Kim tells her mother, well grab a seat at the table so we could talk while

34

I cook breakfast Ms.Pat tells Kim, mommy where daddy at? lil AJ asks Kim, he handling business Kim tells her son and looks at him he looks just like his father Kim tells herself, daddy always handling business mommy lil AJ says I know baby I know Kim replies back.

BANGER

Yo gotti ringtone sounds off, as soon as Banger steps out the shower I'm a real nigga first get money second brake bread with my nigga's we like family so respect it, Banger snatchs up the phone and looks at the caller id which reads BH hello? Banger says Banger what's good? baby boy where the fuck you been at? BH asks over the other end of the phone, man I been low tryna get to the money that's where I been why what's good? Banger says nah nothing much, the home girl got killed yesterday and I'm tryna see if any-body might of heard about who was behind it BH tells Banger, nah bruh I ain't even been around nobody or I haven't been in the hood I been making ot trip's lately Banger tells BH lying but what home-girl got killed and where at? Banger asks, Rain got killed in home-base BH replies back damn Banger thinks to himself Rain was a cool chick and she was bad is hell if she wasn't gay Banger would have tried her on the low because the rules of their set was you couldn't fuck with the home-girl's unless you were tryna marry them, an Banger wasn't tryna do that that's fuck up they killed her but I'll keep my ear's to the street's and let my lil homies know to do the same Banger tells BH, that's what's up lil bruh but I also called you to let you know that I'm gonna have a meeting over the situation so be on standby I'm not gonna tell nobody where it's at until it's ready because some body inside gotta be telling them pigs where we be having our meetings at it's no way for them to run down three times back to back like that and we change up the location each time BH says word up bruh somebody telling Banger replies back, yo another thing BH says just before hanging up the phone, I just cop some more grams of work I got something real nice for you, aight bruh we'll get up as soon as I come outside I just got out the shower Banger says with his mind running with a plan now being as Banger let the two Det.'s tap his phone and put a camera in his hat, he could get Banger on camera giving him the work and that should keep the two Det.'s off his ass for some time, oh yeah lil bruh last thing BH goes on you got 5star now being as ya lil homies stay in line and they always follow calls I'm moving you up, an you keep doing what you doing i'll talk to AJ and see if you could get that g I can't give you the g because that's all I got AJ the only one that could give you the g because he got the double, Banger looks at the phone BH has really lost his mind or he must be high off something BH never talk reckless of the phone like this but it all work in Banger favor, good look big bruh I won't let you down Banger tells BH I know you won't I love you lil bruh hit me as soon as you you get in the hood I'm waiting for AJ to come get me now I might be with him by the time you get outside I'm a just have the work with me, I'm not gonna tell AJ doe because you know how he be bitching about riding dirty with drugs an shit but he always has his gun in the car in the box, he always talking bout the police dog can smell out drugs not guns but fuck him I'll have it on me hit me lil bruh love you BH says again damn Banger thinks to himself whatever BH took he should always take before he calls me the more reckless he talks over the phone the more of a case the Det.'s can put together on not only BH, but also AJ love you back Banger replies ...

NA-JAY&FAT-KAT

Yoo I'm out front bruh Fat-kat say ight here I come Na-jay replies back, bay I'm out Na-jay tells his girlfriend Tae-tae well can I have some money please she responds back what? I just gave you 350 dollars yesterday Na-jay says I spend it you know what keep your money Tae-tae tells Na-jay yo look this is another 350 dollars Na-jay tells Tae-tae and passes her the money and where are you going? that you need money anyway? Na-jay asks my cousin Rain got killed yesterday so I'm going to her mother house the family gonna be their their then we going to the block where she was killed at Tae-tae tells him, so you need money for that Na-jay replies back not really but we might wanna drink and get some food you know how us black people get when one of our people's get killed Tae-tae say yeah I know give me a kiss Na-jay says ight love you na an be safe out there please baby

Tae-tae says I got my safe right here Na-jay tells Tea-tea and show her his 45 pistol Na-jay makes his way thru the house and the name Rain comes to his mind as he walks out the front door to Fat-kat srt-8 jeep, Na-jay knows he heard the name Rain before I'll just ask Fat-kat I know if anybody heard of some body he did bruh what's the shit Na-jay asks Fat-kat once he's inside the jeep, you already know phantom gang Fat-kat replies back phantom gang is Na-jay and Fat-kat set Na-jay went to la to get the green light to start it the reason why he called it phantom was because Na-jay always thought he move like a ghost which phantom means but Na-jay really moved like a young reckless fool, yo kat you ever heard of some chick by the name of Rain? Na-jay asks Rain I think so why you ask? Fat-kat replies my lady said that was her cousin and she got killed yesterday Na-jay tells him Rain you said right? yeah I heard of a Rain but she (tp) and she always on that block they call home-base Fat-kat says Na-jay thoughts are all over the place about this situation something just doesn't feel right about the situation, yo go through the hood so we could talk to black, I hope them young boyz he sent to watch that block ain't go over their and kill that girl Na-jay says to Fat-kat, the look Fat-kat gives Na-jay tells him he think he might just be right.

JABB & YOUNG

Yeah that right young tells his cousin over the phone, I went through your so called headquarters homebase yesterday and shot that shit up me and my homies, young cousin Jabb is apart of (tp) and he lives and would die for (tp) ight don't worry about it I'm a come smoke all of your homies and if I find you I'm a kill you to Jabb tells Young, damn Jabb we family you'll kill me that's fuck up Young replies back nah you fuck up by telling me y'all killed my homegirl Rain and when I see you or any of them phantom bitch ass nigga's it's on, (tp) the fuck up click Jabb is now on fire he walks around his room tryna put a plan together ight I'm about to call big bruh first then I'm a move out first on my cousin then on the rest of them fool's Jabb tells himself as he dail's his big bruh Banger phone number.

CHAPTER 9

V-nasty house

A ll this is so nice all my kids here at my house at one time and we having breakfast V-nasty says as a family should Kintahe says who is V-nasty husband mom you damn sure still know how to cook Krazy J tells his mother from his seat at the table, boy watch your damn mouth at my table before you be eating that food outside, V-nasty tells Krazy J, alright ma Krazy J replies back, Bar-man puts on a kool-aid smile because his mother just check Krazy J, Krazy J gives Bar-man a look that tells him after breakfast I'm a beat you up, which Krazy J always does when he comes to his mother house, he calls it getting Bar-man ready for the street's which Bar-man has no plan's of ever being in, as the family eats all but AJ due to him being so sad over the situation with Kim, she never left the house without telling him, AJ knows he truly fuck-up and when he sees Vickie he might just let Krazy J kill her.

10 MINS LATER V-NASTY HOUSE LIVING ROOM

So ma what's going on with my lil brother an lil sister's AJ asks and then look at each of them this is nothing new AJ always acts like he is his brother's and sister's father, it's no disrespect to their stepfather Kintahe but it's been this way scent their father Jerome left them, oh for the most part everyone is good but this young fast sister of yours Qyanazia, V-nasty says ma I'm not fast Qyanazia says back in her own defense well why you always coming home in the morning

38

Bar-man blurts out Qyanazia gives him a look that could kill if it was capable of doing so oh so miss thang wanna be out all night playing Krazy J says I don't be out playing nothing Qyanazia says back hold, hold I got it AJ tells everyone in the room and look each person over, Kintahe just sits back an let AJ do his thing because at the end of the day he's not any of their father in the room, ma why you ain't call me and let me know about this AJ question his mother AJ listen you and your krazy ass brother are in the street's which I don't approve of but I don't wanna take neither of your focus off watching out for the police or them gangster's because this thang Qyanazia wanna run the street's day an night I got something for her fast ass V-nasty tells AJ ma I'm not fast Qyanazia says again in her defense, shut up while mommy talking Bar-man says, after a few more minutes the family meeting is now over, AJ an Krazy J hug their love ones and make their way out the front door, AJ wait up Qwae-ma tells him, what's good lil momma AJ asks I need to talk to you an J but not in the house Qwae-ma replies back ight come on AJ tells her once all three of them are in the car Qwae-ma goes into the story of what happen on her way home yesterday, Qwae-ma thought long and hard about if she should tell her brother's about what happen but the way that man D-low disrespected her she hopes he gets all he deserves and more from her brother's what Qwae-ma ain't know was that her brother's knew who she was talking about but they both acted as they didn't because they ain't want Qwae-ma to know what was to come of the situation for D-low.

D-LOW

Lil momma that was the best sex I had in along time, D-low tells the under age girl who puts on a kool-aid smile, she's just happy to bring pleasure to her over-age boy friend D-low what this 15 years old girl don't know is D-low has a thing for pretty young girl's only a few people know this about D-low and that's how D-low got his name D-low because he always tryna keep this secret on the low is what he tells everybody who knows about it because he knows if it ever got out he'll be in jail in no time or one of these under age girls father would kill his ass, mookie come on I gotta drop you off home, D-low tells his lil girl-friend I thought you said we could go shopping? lil mookie ask D-low nah lil momma I gotta make some runs real quick I'll take you tomorrow D-low tells her why can't I go with you then we could go shopping after you a done lil mookie is know fool she knows once she gets drop off she won't see D-low for at least another week, lil momma you know you can't be seem with me what would people think? D-low tells lil mookie you could tell them I'm your lil cousin mookie replies back this lil bitch putting up a fight about this shopping shit after tonight I'm cutting this one off fuck how tight she is I'm not blowing my money on know bitch D-low tells himself.

NA-JAY-FAT-KAT

Yoo Black come here Na-jay tells Black from the passenger side of the jeep what's moving big bruh? Black asks Na-jay and goes into their set hand shake once he gets to the jeep, Fat-kat what's good bro? Black asks Fat-kat you know the shit lil bruh Fat-kat replies back yo get in Na-jay tells Black, once Black gets into the back seat Fat-kat pulls off, yo where we going? Black asks because never before have Na-jay and Fat-kat told him to go with them and leave the block with no one to oversee the block, after a minute of no one answering him back Black starts to grab his 38-special off his right-side hip, Black who did you have go watch that block across town? Na-jay asks him what block Black replies back hand still holding on to the gun, home-base 20th ave Na-jay says, oh I ad lil young, Pete, shooter, an ty go over their why what happen? Black asks do you know that them lil fool's went over their and shot the block up I told you to just have them watch the spot nothing else Na-jay tells Black that's what I told them to do big bruh that's my word Black replies back ight if that's your word call young being as he the one with the most status outta them four I know for a fact that they ain't start shooting unless he told them too, now call that lil nigga Na-jay tells Black again ight hold on bruh Black say.

CHAPTER 10

Young

I'm young an Im gettin it the meek millz ringtone goes off and young answer the phone without looking at the caller id what it do big bruh? Young asks Black, Young knows it's Black because he has the ringtone set up for him, you know the shit but where you at lil bruh Black asks Young I'm at my house why what's good? young replies back nah the bigger bruh's wanna holla at you Black tells Young, ight I'm home you know where I live at young tells Black, ight we'll be there in 5 minutes Black says aight I'll be outside in front of the house waiting then Young replies, cool Black says an end the call, Young thoughts are everywhere right now what could the bigger bruh's want Young knows they couldn't of found out about the shooting yesterday because he only told his cousin and his cousin is (tp) their is no-way the bruh's found out from Jabb and the other three bruh's know better to run their mouth about a shooting to anybody because you can't trust anyone anymore that's why Young grab his tec-9 and tuck it under his shirt.

NA-JAY FAT-KAT & BLACK

Pull up right there that's lil young right their Black tells both Na-jay an Fat-kat, Fat-kat rolls down the driver window yo Young get in on my side Fat-kat tells Young, Young diddy bop on his way to the jeep, what's poppin with y'all Young asks as he gets into the jeep back driver side, nothing much Fat-kat replies back to him while Na-jay and Black do their set handshake with Young, so what's this meeting about Young asks because he wanted to get right down to the reason of them coming to get him because if the two bigger bruh's wanted to holla at you one of two thing's was due to change for the good or the bad lil bruh the order Black gave to you about that block homebase what was that order Na-jay ask Young as Fat-kat pull off from in front of Young house on Chadwick and Avon, oh black told me to be on the watch for AJ, BH and AJ brother silly J, so what happen? Na-jay asks Young, Young looks to Black for him to shoot him some bell, but Black is face looking out the back passenger side window me Pete, shooter an ty went around their, we were straight up mobin then we saw their homie Bear I guess he oversee that block because he always on the look-out when ever I go through their, but anyway then we see the dude BH so now we all ready for war and shit young says, ight go on Na-jay tells Young, Young look to Black again but Black still haven't look Young way yet, so boom right young goes on they were walking and we rode past them an they were all looking krazy at the car but we know they can't see us because the tint's on the windows but shooter gets mad and tells Pete to spin the block, I'm like nah they on to us, but ty ain't listen to me young says, hold on so you telling us that you got the highest status in the car and they ain't listen to you Fat-kat asks young big bruh when we together we don't be of that status shit we all brother's, noone is the highest we all one when we together Young replies back, lil bruh get to the story Na-jay tells Young, ight so we spin the block an shit and now we coming toward them an it's three of them now two dude's an a chick Ty said it look like BH was reaching so you know my reaction timing big bruh be on point so I started banging first out the sunroof because that was open and my window would had took to long to roll down Young says, so you saying nobody ain't start shooting first Na-jay ask nah but they were reaching and if Ty said they were they were in my book Young replies, so who all know about it other then now us three and the three that was with you, because that chick that was with BH an Bear on that block was killed yesterday an her name is Rain Fat-kat tells Young, awww we killed a bitch that had to be Shooter work because my gun don't kill women or kids Young replies, but for the most part the only person that know about it is my cousin Jabb Young tells them in the jeep, Jabb Na-jay asks yeah Jabb he my cousin Young says well how does he know if he wasn't in the car with you when it happen Fat-kat asks Young knows he has talk himself in some shit by letting them know his cousin knew but he rather get dp then have to kill his cousin he really rather they kill Jabb because going up against Jabb was not something Young wanted to do an Young knew what Jabb said to him he meant it, big bruh I slip up and told him because he family I'll take the dp for it Young says, Fat-kat just shakes his head these young dudes these days telling people things that could get them 100 years nah lil bruh where your cousin at? we just gonna bring him home under the set Na-jay says big bruh he not gonna be with it Young tells Na-jay how you know that? Na-jay asks Black just sits in the backseat an shakes his head an look looks out the window, what is he? Na-jay asks Young he tp Young tells him and puts down his head which was the second dumbest thing he did in his life the first was telling his cousin about them shooting up home-base Na-jay turns in his seat with the quickness and put two bullets in Young head boom, boom man push that fool out the car Black when we get on 10st on the graveyard block …

LU & T-DUB

Look t I'm telling you bro I know the person who's the top dawg of that tp shit me and him did time down northern state gang unit I'm a tell him you family poppy and I brought you where you belong he has respect for the nation Lu tells T-dub fuck him he just like the rest of them black's they all big headed and think they run everything, T-dub has been tryna get lu not to talk to the old man because once he talk to the old man and the old man reach out to AJ and them and they told him T-dub ran off with 100 bricks and switch the old man was gonna relay that back to Lu who would want T-dub to break bread with the nation because T-dub was putting the brother's life at risk or Lu would have T-dub give the work back, Lu already told one of the brother's who is down Rahway state prison with the old man to go tell him he

needed to talk to him because it could be a all out war, so any minute
they should be calling in T-dub mind he prayed they didn't call, the
pit-bull ringtone goes off, here they go right here Lu tells T-dub hello?
hey poppy Lu a female voice over the other end of the cell phone says
hey mommy what's going on? Lu asks nothing much I got Joey over
the other end he told me to call you, the female says alright mommi
join the call Lu replies ok poppy the female says real sexy, yoo brother
what's good? Joey ask nothing much just tryna get by Lu tells Joey I
hear you bro I hear you but I got your friend old man right here I'm
about to put him on the line Joey tells Lu ok Lu tells Joey while placing
the phone on speaker and sitting it on the table so T-dub could hear
the conversation also, lu what's good bruh? how's life treating you?
the old man ask once he's on the phone all is good brother other then
this lil situation that just took place I hate I have to reach out to you
about this matter we should be talking about better things you know
bro? Lu says Lu it ain't about nothing what's the situation about? the
old man asks my lil cousin was running with your family at one point
but they weren't showing him no love so I took him into the nation Lu
speaks in code's because he knows the police might be tune in to this
phone call, ight so what's the problem the old man asks again well two
of your lil one's came and tried to sent him off over the situation Lu
tells the old man what's their names who came through? the old mad
ask their names are AJ and krazy I think t what's the brother name Lu
asks T Krazy J T tells Lu oh his name is Krazy J, Lu tells the old man,
well Lu you are right those two are mines but for them to try and move
on your cousin over him not being with my family any-more is under
them that's not them you sure your cousin ain't do no food shit the
old man says because he for one knows AJ is not gonna kill someone
because they switch that goes on everyday, Lu looks to T, T you didn't
do nothing right beside switch over Lu asks T-dub, T-dub shakes his
head to his older cousin no poppy, bro my lil cousin said that's all he
has done nothing more nothing less, Lu says to the old man, Lu just
hold off on sending your people out to move I'm asking you outta the
love and respect we have for each other I'm a call my lil one's and see
about this situation and I'll have your man's right here with me hit

you back but if he can't get through to you for whatever reason I'll be home monday and I'll come holla at you myself deal? the old man says to Lu ok deal poppy and you could have told me you were about to be free I would have had some mommi's come pick you up from prison Lu tells the old man, nah I'm good lu but I'm a hit you the old man replies, ight Lu says an ends the call see everything work out T just like I told you Lu says yeah but I don't trust him T-dub says he's my man's and I trust him Lu says getting upset because T-dub doesn't trust his judgement ok Lu you got it T-dub says thank you T now let's hit the block Lu tells T-dub.

KIM

Ma that breakfast is what I needed Kim tells her mother, I see you ate all that food like you haven't ate in day's what you eating for two? Kim mother Ms.Pat asks what? ma why you ask that? Kim asks her mother Ms.Pat no I was just playing Ms.Pat says grandma that food was good lil AJ tells Ms.Pat thank you grandbaby Ms.Pat replies Kim father just sits back and drinks his coffee and watches Kim movement he still haven't question Kim about what's going on? well now that everybody is done eating everybody out my kitchen so I could clean up, Ms.Pat tells everybody at the table, ma I'll help you Kim tells Ms.Pat, know baby girl I got it you lil AJ and your father go into the living-room I could handle this on my own Ms.Pat says ok miss independent Kim Joes with her moms while leaving out the kitchen with lil AJ and her father, mommy can I go play with my toys in the other room lil AJ asks Kim go-head Kim replies once lil AJ is out the room Joe goes right in on Kim with the question baby girl what's going on with you? what do you mean? Kim replies, you over here without AJ and you talking about staying a few days I might not be the smartest man on the earth but I know a problem when I see one Joe says dad I'm not gonna lie I been going thru alot as of lately with AJ stressing me out all the time running the street's and with this daycare not coming together how I want it to is just more stress added and daddy I'm pregnant again Kim tells her father breaking down crying, Joe goes to his baby girl and wrap his arms around her, it's gonna be alright baby girl I'm here for you, have you told AJ? Joe asks no daddy he doesn't know and I don't even know if I want to keep the baby, Kim says what girl you not killing no baby that ain't ask to be here, Kim father Joe is a god fearing man and he knows killing a baby is a big sin, daddy you gotta understand it's just a lot right now and I don't know what to do Kim tells Joe, Kim when you met and married AJ you knew who and what he was and that was a street guy so now you gotta live with it, but just know every man time comes when he's ready to stop running the street's let's just pray it's by his choice and no one else's meaning killer's or the police, baby girl I'm a have a talk with AJ man to man Joe says no daddy I don't want you to do that it's my problem's Kim says alright I won't call him Joe says but is lying to Kim as soon as he finds the time away from Kim he's gonna call AJ and have a talk with him.

AJ & KRAZY J

Big bruh that's fucked up how Kim left the house without telling you Krazy J tries to gas the situation between Kim and AJ but AJ doesn't pay his lil brother no attention, AJ drives the black machine down the parkway toward Newark, yo call that fool BH AJ tells Krazy J ight Krazy J replies, yoo what's good krazy where y'all at? BH ask yeah we getting off the parkway now, Krazy J says where y'all want me to meet y'all at? BH asks tell him meet us on 19th ave an 22nd street AJ tells Krazy J, yo big bruh said meet us on 19th ave an 22nd st aint know police around their right Krazy J says nah they just sitting on home-base but I'm about to start walking toward that way now BH say cool we'll meet you there in 3mins Krazy J replies …

CHAPTER 11

5 mins later

Damn Krazy move your seat up some BH tells Krazy J as he gets into the back seat of the passenger side of the black machine, fool you fucking up my groove Krazy J replies while lifting up his seat, the three man do their set hand-shake, so what happen yesterday AJ asks as he pulls off heading toward 18th ave and 22nd st man shit got real yesterday I'm a tell y'all the story but go thru 18th an 18th so I could get some weed from baby an them BH say yo where baby at BH question one of the young gunner's on 18th ave an 18th street through the back passenger window it depends who wanna know one of the young dude's says to BH lil nigga you must not know who I am I'll fuck ya lil ass up BH tells the young kid man you not gonna do shit to me I'm 118 the young kid replies, yo what's the problem? Baby ask while coming out from the blue trap house on 18th st ya lil homie was bout to get it that's the problem BH tells Baby you wasn't bout to do nothing the young boy says out loud, yo chill lil bruh this my mans baby tells the younin yo BH what could I do for you baby ask while approaching the car first you could let me beat that lil young dude ass then let me get a oz of that fire weed BH say I could help you with the second thing but the first thing you not touching my lil bruh Baby replies, ight just let me get my weed so we could get off this hot ass block BH says ight hold on young pusher go get that oz for me Baby tells one of his lil homies, yo AJ Krazy J what it do? Baby asks the brother's nothing much AJ responds back while Krazy

J just nods his head up and down, here you go big bruh young pusher says while handing the weed to Baby, Baby then hands the weed to BH through the open window how much? BH ask 350 dollar's Baby tells BH 350 dollar's BH shouts this some bull shit baby I could go across town and get it for lower then this BH says well go head Baby says while reaching back for the weed, nah I'm a keep it I just hope this shit fire BH tells Baby while handing baby the 350 dollars from outta his pants pocket ight Baby be safe AJ tells baby putting the car in drive y'all two baby replies stepping off, yo I ate them nigga's BH says once they pulled off I should had robbed them, yo break some of that weed off and put the rest in the box behind the seat Krazy J tells BH oh shit Krazy J you tryna get smart o a nigga BH says it ain't about being smart I'm just not tryna go to jail today for no dumbass weed Krazy J say yeah lil bruh right AJ agree with Krazy J so now it'd team up on BH day y'all two nigga's kill me BH say.

BANGER

Lil bruh what's moving? Banger ask Jabb as soon as Jabb gets into the car, big bruh did the hood get shot up yesterday Jabb asks Banger looks at Jabb while he rides up avon toward 17th st yeah why you know something about it? because a homegirl by name Rain got killed Banger says yeah I know something about it my cousin young he phantom he called my house bragging how he shot the headquarters up but I ain't know a homegirl got killed but I told him I was gonna kill him whenever I see him, then he started talking this family shit but tp my family I love my set fuck everybody who ain't with us Jabb says Banger is not surprise by Jabb words the gangs have took over every-one mind making them think this is all they have and all that matters in life, word up lil bruh Banger replies word up is all that Banger can think of to say for about the way Jabb feel's, os lil bruh where you want me to drop you off at? Banger asks let me out at 20th an avon I'm about to go through home-base and see the bruh's Jabb says ...

LOCATION PATHMARK AJ KRAZY J & BH

Man you got us meeting up with this bitch ass nigga Krazy J says to BH, bruh he the homie and everybody not a gangster he knows how to make money and all his lil homies follow his lead BH tells Krazy J man he stills a bitch Krazy J says yo both of y'all chill out AJ tells both BH an Krazy J while he search the parking lot for anything outta place AJ doesn't know why but he feels something is not right, there he goes right their Krazy J says while pointing to Banger infiniti g37 as it pulls into the parking lot, Banger spot's AJ black 760 bmw and he pulls into the empty parking spot next to the black machine, look at his bitch ass Krazy J says out loud BH go handle whatever business you have with him in his car AJ says I was already gonna do that BH tells himself what AJ or Krazy J don't know is BH had the motherload on him crack and pills ight I'll just be 2 minutes top BH tells them exiting the car, unlock the door Banger BH says oh my bad big bruh my mind was somewhere else Banger tells BH well you need to get your mind on this money BH tells Banger they go into their set hand shake then go right into business yo Banger this a bird I'm a put it under my seat and this is a 100 e-pills I know people don't really fuck with them to much being as molly's took over but just give me two dollars a pill and break the bird down between all your block's and me and you share whatever you bring back 50-50 you could keep your so call buy money this a front is what you could take it as BH tells Banger

being as Banger is really soft he doesn't even put up a fight about it he just goes on like the yes man he is, so you got that what I just told you BH ask, what? yeah yeah I got you bruh Banger says are you alright? BH ask Banger yeah I'm good bruh I just got alot on my mind Banger replies, far as what you beefing with somebody let me know because I could use my g status to get whoever you want touch BH say nah bruh it's nothing like that, oh yeah I found out where that hit came from Banger say word up who? BH ask gas up some young dude name young he phantom my lil homie Jabb said it's his cousin and he called Jabb bragging about the shit my lil homie said even though it's his cousin he was gonna handle him Banger tells BH and you believe him

BH ask with his face twisted up, bruh my lil homie loves the set and nothing else not even his mother Banger says see that's why I'm a get that g status for you I'm a talk to bruh about that as soon as I get back into the car BH says you ain't gotta do that I'm good with my 5 star Banger says what bruh you bugging you deserve it BH tells Banger if only you knew Banger thinks to himself the only thing I deserve is to be killed for being a rat.

CHAPTER 12

Tommy and Big-dawg

Big-dawg I'm telling you I gotta cut AJ and them off our people who we have on the inside hit me and told me he on the watch list, Tommy tells Big-dawg cousin listen just because he on the watch list don't me nothing long as he use his chain of command right whoever telling under their set won't be able tie us to them unless it's AJ brother Krazy J or his right hand man's telling which I myself don't think either of them telling Big-dawg says, I know Big-dawg but I just wanna play it safe Tommy replies, what no one knows Tommy and Big-dawg are partner's in both the drug game and also when it comes to their many use car lot's Big-dawg an Tommy sometimes use their car lot's to move drug in and outta state's they not only own the car lot best way on 1&9 but they own car lots through many states and cities Tommy just call our inside man and push up on him to find out who's the rat in their organization them brick's you gave them should hold them for at least 3 weeks top Big-dawg say aight I'm a call him right now Tommy replies.

DET. KILLBURG & DET. JACKSON

Like father like son the rapper the-game ringtone goes off and Det. Jackson answer his phone without looking at his phone he set this ringtone up just for his son Tommy and no one else, what boy? I'm at work Det.Jackson says into the phone, Det.Jackson knows what Tommy does for a living he doesn't like it but every man has his own ways of making money Det.Jackson understands that dad I need you Tommy replies what I'm at a homicide-scene Det.Jackson tells Tommy alright real quick then can you talk for a minute Tommy ask, let me walk off Det.Jackson replies, alright what the hell you want boy? Det.Jackson ask, dad one of my people on the watch list I ain't tell you I knew him when you first said the name the other day but that's one of my peoples and I need to know who's telling on him so me and him can start back getting to the money Tommy says, ok I hear you boy but what's the name of this business partner you have? Det.Jackson ask Det.Jackson told his son Thomas Jackson the 2nd some many people name's on the watch list that he doesn't remember all the name's Det.Jackson only reason for telling Tommy the name's was so Tommy wouldn't deal with somebody on the watch list, his name is AJ dad Tommy says what? Det.Jackson yells and then looks around to make sure know one was watching him, Tommy me and my partner are working on that guy AJ case and we were looking to bring him and anybody else down with him, matter a fact I'm on one of his block's home-base is what they call it Det.Jackson tells Tommy why are you over their for? Tommy asks his father while giving Big-dawg a look that says things are not looking good well some girl got killed and we shut the block down Det.Jackson say damn Tommy thinks to himself he hopes AJ or his shot-caller Bear is good because he haven't heard from either of them scent he gave them the bricks of dope, they usually would have called an said the dope was good or not, dad can you please help me on this one he's my people and I got love for him it's not just about money with me and him, we made a tight relationship Tommy tells his father, ok boy this the last time I'm a help you out Det.Jackson says while looking around to see if anybody could hear him, his name is rome davis but he goes by Banger Det.Jackson tells Tommy ok dad good looking out love you Tommy says love you back son Det.Jackson replies click, Det.Jackson turns around to see who was calling him, yeah Det.Killburg? Det. Jackson says who was that the wife Det.Killburg ask, no that was my son Det.Jackson replies oh how is he doing Det.Killburg ask oh he's doing better now Det.Jackson says hey that's all that matter how bout we get up outta here and head to the precinct let's see if our boy Banger show up with some thing and see what he knows about this killing Det.Killburg says that sound like a plan to me Det.Jackson tells Det.Killburg with his thought still on his son Det.Jackson also hopes his partner or no one else ever found out who his son was or what he did for a living because if it came out Det.Jackson and Tommy would be in some deep shit.

NA-JAY & FAT-KAT

That taco-bell food hit the spot Na-jay says to Fat-kat who is eating his last taco, damn Black you really aint want nothing to eat Fat-kat ask Black, nah I'm good bruh black says, aww I hope seeing a dead body ain't stop you from eating Na-jay says testing black gangster what neither Na-jay or Fat-kat know is Black really had love for young like a real brother and for them to kill him and leave him on the side of the road like that was fucked up yo Black we about to drop you of in the hood Fat-kat says ight that's cool Black tells Fat-kat while all types of thoughts are running through Black's mind, Black truly want to kill both Na-jay and Fat-kat right now but he knows if he fuck up they not only gonna kill him but also his family, what Black don't know is Fat-kat is already two steps ahead of him he's been watching Black scent Na-jay first shot young and Black mood haven't been the same, but it's nothing to Fat-kat he already has plan in his mind to kill Black at the next meeting the three of them have together.

5 MINUTES LATER

Black call me later on Na-jay tells black once they pull up on Osborne Terr, which is their headquarters for phantom, ight big bruh I'm a hit you black says while getting out the jeep without doing their set hand-shake, but in black mind he knew this was the last time either of them would see him on this side of town again unless he was killing them black had plan's to call his big cousin baby up from 18th an 18th and switch his hood, once black is out the jeep Fat-kat takes off, kat what you think about black mood change after I push young Na-jay says bruh you saw how he started acting after you smoke young we gotta off him asap Fat-kat say that's what we gonna do but we gotta do it some-time next week because once they find young body shit gonna be hot and if we kill black now it's gonna look like we cleaning house under our hood, and we don't need to be getting blame for nobody's Na-jay says wee we work the best as a team love you bruh Fat-kat says love you more bruh Na-jay replies.

CHAPTER 13

Kim 3:30 pm

Mom I told you, you didn't have to cook you already made breakfast now lunch ma you doing the most right now Kim tells her mother Ms.Pat girl you eating for two now so you need all the food you can get Ms.Pat says yeah mommy the baby in you gotta eat to lil AJ say after cleaning up the kitchen Kim mother walked into the living room and caught Joe holding Kim who was crying her eye's out and after getting a update from both Kim and Joe that Kim was pregnant Kim mother has been going overboard taken care of Kim every want and need I'm a start dinner right after Ms.Pat says ma you don't have to Kim says, Kim you're wasting your time you know your mother gonna do what she want to do so let's just go back in the living room and watch some reruns of the jamie foxx show, Joe say your right daddy Kim says while walking out the kitchen.

D-LOW
Baby what's good bruh? D-low ask baby while he sits pulled over on 18th ave an 18th st you know the shit D-low what's good? baby say yo let me get one of them fat dub'z you got D-low says Baby drop's the 20 of weed on the passenger seat and s-low hands him the money, Baby quickly count's the money, yo this only 18 dollars D-low baby say come on baby you tripping over two dollar's I thought you were bigger than two dollar's Baby D-low replies Dawg it's not about what I'm bigger than it's my money you should have told me you were short

Baby say ight whatever D-low says whatever what? Baby ask, D-low you keep playing with me I'm a knock you the fuck out Baby tells D-low you got it Baby D-low says bitching up asap because he knows Baby would really knock him out, next time tell me you short baby tells D-low and steps off you got that one for now D-low says to no one but himself.

V-NASTY

Girl where the hell you think you going? V-nasty questions Qyanazia ma I'm going out with one of my friend Qyanazia tells her mother friend which friend? V-nasty ask ma you don't know him but he's cool people's Qyanazia says cool people's my ass V-nasty tells Qyanazia, why don't you just stay home today with the family V-nasty husband Kintahe tells Qyanazia, Qyanazia shoots him a dirty look, Qyanazia and Kintahe has been beefing scent V-nasty and Kintahe got together Qyanazia feel's that Kintahe is the reason behind V-nasty and her father not being together no-more and what did your brother's just tell you at breakfast you gotta be careful of the guys you going out with because if they got beef with my two boy'z there'll do a sucker move and try to hurt one of us instead of going after them V-nasty tells Qyanazia you know what ma I'm not even gonna go out today, I'll just stay the weekend, in my room Qyanazia says and walk off to her room and gives Kintahe the evil eye, that girl of your V, I'm telling you one of these days it's gonna be me and her one on one Kintahe tells V-nasty Kintahe if you wish to put a hand on her be my guest but just know her brother's gonna have your head in a new york minute V-nasty says, well my head might just be worth beating her grown ass Kintahe replies well go on facebook and start a account so people can help me with your funeral.

JABB

Lil momma why you crying so hard she gone but we'll never forget her Jabb tells the dark skin female who's crying her eyes out she was my first cousin we grew up together we did everything together

I mean everything the female tells Jabb, what's your name? Jabb asks the female, my name is Tae-tae the female says well Tae-tae my name is Jabb I know you don't know me but Rain was my home-girl I fucked with sis hard and I promise you I'm a kill everybody who had something to do with killing her, Jabb tells Tae-tae you said that just now like you know who did it? Tae-tae question Jabb, baby girl I'm not one for running my mouth to female's about gangster shit but being as you Rain cousin, all I'm a tell you is them phantom nigga's did it Jabb replies, who did it? Tae-tae ask Jabb Tae-tae heard Jabb the first time but she wanna make sure she heard Jabb right, I said them phantom fool's did it Jabb tells Tae-tae again and how do you know for sure Tae-tae questions Jabb again let's just say I know what I know and that's all I know, Jabb replies well Jabb let me tell you and ask you for something, I'm a start by telling you I'm not a hoe and I don't run around pushing up on dudes now what I wanna ask you for is your number so we could talk and if I hear anything about who did this to my cousin I'll call you and let you handle your business and if you hear anything let me know Tae-tae tells Jabb ight we could do that I was type feeling you anyway but I ain't wanna just come out and ask you for your number because of what you going through with losing your cousin Jabb says it's already Tae-tae say while pulling out her iphone some they could exchange phone number's, while exchanging numbers with Jabb Tae-tae is making plan's in her mind to try and get some information outta Na-jay and if she founded out Na-jay had something to do with her cousin killing she Tae-tae was gonna set him up, Tae-tae is no fool if anybody knows something dealing with phantom it's Na-jay because after all he always tells her that's his set and he's the big homie of phantom, Jabb thoughts are also running wild but his is about sexing Tae-tae Jabb already knows who put the work in to kill Rain but that's not something he wants to share because saying names is a sign of an snitch …

CHAPTER 14

Old-man AJ, BH & Krazy J

You have a prepaid call from da-don to accept this call push one to, yoo AJ what's good lil bruh the old man says once the call is join together, nothing much bruh just making these rounds picking up this money from the bruh's AJ replies oh yeah who you with? the old man asks my brother krazy ass and BH AJ says put the phone on speaker the old man says you on speaker already AJ tells the old man, what's good with the brother's? the old man asks you know the shit Krazy J says all is well BH responds while rolling up another blunt, Imiss y'all nigga's the Old-man tells all three of them, awww your old ass getting soft Krazy J say lil bruh I'm the hardest gangster you'll ever meet in this life and in the next lifetime the old man replies yeah that's what all y'all old school punks say Krazy J tells the old man meaning every word, I'm a fuck your lil ass up when I see you lil j, the old man says I ain't lil j no-more Krazy J replies yeah whatever lil j, but BH how's it looking the old man says, all is good big bruh we just waiting for you to get home that's all BH replies, hold up, yo why you even calling for you come home tomorrow I told you we'll be their to get you nobody ain't forget about you so calling us to remind us right now what's that gonna do? AJ I'm not calling about that I'm calling because somebody I did time with and became cool with reached out to me about a situation that got you and Krazy J name in it the old man says what is it? AJ ask hold on I'm a tell you, you and your lil brother suppose to had tried to make a movie on some body name T, and? Krazy J says

58

getting real heated, J cool out AJ tells his brother big bruh go head finish AJ tells the old man, like I was saying before big mouth cut me off the dude t is my man's lil cousin and he said he was with our family but switch to fuck with that poppy nation, ou know what I mean, the old man tells AJ, yeah I know what you talking about AJ replies now my mans said you and your brother tried to make a movie outta him because of that, I told my man's that's under the both of you to make a move over because somebody switched, lil bru from me to you is so let dude be, because dudes switch their hood everyday the old man tells AJ, ight now hear me out your mans lil cousin t who we know as T-dub ran off with a 100 breeze'zz we never knew he switch but now it adds up he with the poppy's AJ replies, lil bruh my mans ain't tell me that but best bet my mans don't know about his lil cousin doing that, from what I know of my mans he would had made his cousin give the work back because he don't like to go to war, not that he's pussy or nothing it's just he loves living life and making money and you can't do either at war but I'm a hit my mans and let him know but if I can't get through to him today we'll just go through north Newark when I get out tomorrow and holla at him the old man says that's cool bruh we'll see you tomorrow a,j says love y'all the old man says love you to bruh all the man in the car say at the same time an end the call so would one of you please update me on this situation because I'm lost BH tells the brother's Krazy J tell BH what happen yesterday AJ says ight so it happen like this Krazy J says ...

BANGER

Hey Ms.William is Det.Jackson or Det.Killburg here, Banger asks the old police office at the front desk of the police station, hold on, no they are not in they signed out hours ago, Ms.William tells Banger after checking the sign out book for the officer's but is their anything I could help you with? Ms.William ask Banger Ms.William knows Banger because Det.Killburg and Det.Jackson had him here so much he mind is well truly work for the police be on the payroll an all Banger looks around then, says yeah is ltwhite in because they told me to see him, if they weren't in Banger says I'm a call his office sweetheart hold on, yeah Lt I have Det. Killburg an Det.Jackson snitch is here Ms.William says into the phone put no cut on it when she said it either even know Ms.William is a cop she still dislikes snitches even know they make the police work easy, well Mr. you could go on up to the Lt office I know you know the way by now, Ms.William tells Banger, Banger just put his head down it's nothing he could say to gain any-self respect from her, she knows he's a snitch and in any-one book's snitches don't get no respect from no one …

LT WHITE OFFICE & BANGER

Hey Banger how's it's going Lt.White asks Banger as he opens the office door for him, everything alright Lt I'm just dropping the camera film off from the hat, Banger says alright grab a seat while I plug this thing up to get the film outta it, you want something to drink or anything Lt.White says, no I'm good Banger responds back taking a seat in the black roll chair, did you get anything good on this film Lt.White asks yeah Banger replies well let's watch a lil bit of it together you ain't got nowhere to be right? Lt.White asks, not really Banger replies, alright here we go Lt. White says plugging the tv up and taken a seat behind his desk …

TOMMY & BIG-DAWG

Yo Tommy try to call AJ again we gotta let him know what's he up against Big-dawg tells Tommy, Tommy father Det.Jackson texted Tommy phone and told him that he forgot to tell him Banger is also wearing a camera and his phone is also tap, bruh I tried three time already he must be on the phone or his shit might be dead, Tommy says fuck I told you we should have never started dealing with gang Bangers because it's alway's some bull shit with them Big-dawg say bruh you agreed with me to bring AJ in talking bout he had a army and we could use that Tommy say alright know one is to blame for it let just shoot to Newark and see if we could run into him Big-dawg say alright let's roll but you driving because I hate driving down 1&9 Tommy tells his cousin throwing him the car keys to the gray s550 benz.

QWAE MA- & BAR-MAN

Knock, knock, knock who? Bar-man asks it's me your twin Qwae-ma says from the other side of the door, come in qwae, Bar-man say once inside the bedroom Qwae-ma closest the door and makes her way to have a seat on the bed, Bar-man room is the dirtiest room in the house but that's nothing to Qwae-ma she's used to it, twin I gotta talk to you about something, I think I made a mistake and I feel bad about it Qwae-ma say what you do? Bar-man asks turning the jay-z hard knock life cd off on the radio from Qwae-ma lowering her eye's to the floor, Bar-man knows his lil sister by three minutes of birth truly feel bad about whatever she did, Bar-man you know me and you could talk about any an everything and I know you could keep a secret Qwae-ma say what is it? Bar-man asks the other day I was on my way home from the library and some-guy pulled up on the side of me in a black Audi and got real disrespectful, who is he? Bar-man questions his sister ready to fight who-ever dis his sister, Bar-man listen he got real disrespectful because I wouldn't talk to him and called me all types of names Qwae-ma tells her twin breaking down crying, Qwae-ma it's alright, Bar-man tells her wrapping his arms around her, and I told AJ and j what he said and I know in my heart they gonna kill him if they see the guy but I just hope they don't get into know trouble for it Bar-man, Qwae-ma say Qwae-ma it's a lot of black Audi's in the city, it'll be hard to find him so don't worry about it Bar-man tells Qwae-ma Qwae-ma start's to shake her head side to side, what? Qwae-ma why you shaking your head? Bar-man asks because I told them his name Qwae-ma says and how do you know his name? Bar-man asks because he told me and then pulled off after telling me Qwae-ma replies what's his name? Bar-man asks D-low Qwae-ma replies D-low I heard that name before but I don't remember where Bar-man tells Qwae-ma what neither of them know is D-low is Qyanazia new boyfriend and Bar-man heard the name D-low right here in this house, when Qyanazia was walking out the bath-room one-day she said D-low name walking pass Bar-man.

CHAPTER 15

bad-Tina & Bear

Bear come on, alright you ain't gotta give me a 20 dollar bag of crack to suck you off, I'll just do it for a dime bag, bad-Tina tells Bear ight that'll work step on the side of the house Bear replies Bear you one tight dude I sure wish my boo BH was out here because I knew he would have took care of me with no problem bad-Tina says while walking on the side of the green house with Bear away from the police car's that's still left on the block your boo? Bear knows bad-Tina is the big bruh's first sex partner but calling BH her boo that's something else, well Tina your boo not around so you got me and I'm only giving you a dime bag that's it I'm not into paying for no sex like your boo BH, Bear says that tryna down play BH name what Bear can't understand how BH has a family at home but would rather sleep over Tina house an be sexing her and not his baby mom's, for your info lil Bear bad-Tina replies while dropping to the ground in front of Bear BH don't pay for this mouth or this pussy I don't gotta make him pay we smoke together, y'all smoke what together? Bear asks we smoke crack together bad-Tina say right before putting her mouth on Bear dick.

DET. KILLBURG & DET. JACKSON

Hey Ms.William how's it going? Det.Jackson ask Ms.William the desk office of the precinct, hey Det.Jackson and where is your partner? Ms.William ask I'm right here so you miss me Det.Killburg says to

Ms.William while coming thru the front door of the precinct, oh hey Det.Killburg, Ms.William replied Det.Killburg walked straight pass Ms.William going to his office without speaking to her, Det. Killburg knows Ms.William doesn't like him so he's see's know reason to even act like he likes her, Det.Jackson just looks at his partner some-times he doesn't know how they even get along, I hate that cracker Ms.William tells Det.Jackson breaking his thoughts, I think he also hates you to Det.Jackson replied, but what's going on around here any-news on anything? Det.Jackson asks matter a fact your just in time you and Det. Jackass rat is in the office with Lt. White, Ms.William says how long has he been in their? Det.Jackson ask I'll say about a hour now Ms.William replied damn Det.Jackson says to himself and thinks if him and his partner didn't take that hour lunch break they would have been here when Banger got here, alright thanks Ms.William Det.Jackson tells her you welcome she replies Det.Jackson steps to him an his partner office so he could tell Det. Killburg that Banger is in the building an is in Lt. White office.

KIM & TOYA

Toya I'm so happy I call you my mother was doing the most I had to get out that house Kim tells her best friend Toya, what are friends for if they can't be there for each other Toya replies, word Kim says while walking side by side with her friend through Jersey Garden Mall, but Kim have you called AJ today to at least check on him? Toya ask what? girl he been calling my phone almost every hour I know he's alright and I'm not ready to talk to him and when I do decide to talk to him I hope he's ready to be a father to another person because I'm keeping my baby rather he likes it or not Kim say I know that's right Toya replied.

JOE & AJ

So AJ listen to me and listen to me well your hurting my baby girl you got her stress out an don't you know stress can kill her or hurt the baby she's carrying AJ is caught off guard by this he didn't know

Kim was pregnant but he doesn't say anything to Joe he just let him talk, so AJ you need to tighten up because I'll still fight you old or not I'll fight you over my baby girl AJ, I know you would AJ replied to Joe so AJ handle your business and this phone call is between us I gotta go the wife is calling I gotta go help with dinner Joe says alright pop'z love you AJ says I love you to AJ be safe out there Joe says as he ends the phone call

aww I love you pop'z Krazy J says once AJ is off the phone yo j mind your business AJ says to his brother mind my business you the one on the phone talking around me Krazy J replies word up doe AJ you talking around us it's our business to, BH says y'all got that AJ tells them both while placing his phone in the cup-holder and turing the young jezzy back up to the max ...

CHAPTER 16

Judy & lady

L ady I'm telling you BH was about to kill me, Judy tells her friend Lady, girl you trippin you know that fool loves you lady replied but if you wanna come out here to allentown with me girl come on it ain't like I got nobody here with me in this house Lady says, thanks Lady your the best text me you address so I could put it into the gps on my phone and I'll call you when we halfway to your house Judy say alright I'm about to text you it now an drive safe I'll be waiting for y'all Lady say love you girl Judy tells Lady I love you to girl Lady replied before ending the call Alecia you ready baby? Judy ask her daughter yes mommy Alecia replied ok let's go Judy tells her grabbing her pocketbook, mommy daddy not coming with us? Alecia ask no baby we going to lady house for a while you'll be able to call your father soon as we get their Judy tells Alicia but is truly hoping she forgets about her father not just for now but forever.

6:30 PM NORTH NEWARK

Everyone this meeting is now in so anyone caught talking you already know what it is a cocky short poppy dude tells all his brother's at the meeting alright my brother's Lu says taken over the meeting we just had a meeting yesterday over my lil cousin t getting shot at and we all agreed on going to war, but I use my power an name to reach out to the two guys who came around here to kill my cousin big homie, me an him have a good history report from being in the same prison's together he knows how I gets down and I know how he gets down also the respect goes both ways between us now he said he would check his lil homies and dead the situation because T switching over to the nation shouldn't be a big problem and could be peaced up so we gonna hold off on the war, he's gonna come thru here tomorrow and see me about the situation or he should call me tonight, a tall poppy raises his hand so he could speak, go head poppy you can talk Lu tells him, well all I wanna know do you really trust him? the tall man asks yes Lu tells him without a doubt ok poppy the tall man says, anyone else? Lu asks and turn an look each of the man in the eye's stopping at T T do you have something to say before this meeting ends? Lu ask T looks Lu in the eye's does he knows I took them 100brick's T-dub thinks to himself but the way Lu looks at him tells T that he knows something, nah I ain't got nothing to say T-dub say alright this meeting is over and T make sure you be out early tomorrow just in case they come through I want you on the block with me, meeting with them are you ok with that? Lu asks T-dub I'm good with that Lu T-dub says while his mind is making up a plan so Lu or the brother's won't find out about the brick's he beat AJ and them for which he doesn't have any more.

BANGER

Its late is hell Banger tells himself as he gets into his Infiniti g37 which was parked around the corner from the police station after watching the film with Lt. White over three times because Det.Killburg and Det.Jackson show up and they also wanted Banger to explain everything from the film to the phone conversation with BH, Banger is tried and just wanna go lay up with his jumpoff Tt, before Banger pulled off a thought hit him why was Det.Jackson looking at him like that Det.Jackson eye's was on Banger more than the film they were watching, Banger doesn't know what to make of the situation so he just shakes it off and pulls off heading to north Munn to Tt house.

D-LOW & QYANAZIA

So what you saying lil momma you not coming out tonight? D-low asks Qyanazia no my moms on some bull shit talking about me messing with guys that my brother's might be beefing with Qyanazia replied, what's your brother's name and how many do you have? D-low asks I got three brother's for their names that's a story for another day and don't really matter because I'm grown Qyanazia replies, you right lil momma they name's don't matter what matter is our relationship D-low tells her tryna shoot some game but just hit me tomorrow and we could chill D-low tells Qyanazia tryna rush her off the phone now because she couldn't come out so in D-low mind he was wasting his time talking to her, but I wanna stay up all night and talk to you Qyanazia tells D-low, ma I gotta handle some business so I'll hit you tomorrow click the phone call ends, Qyanazia falls back onto her bed, I hate my life Qyanazia yells out loud to herself, for D-low the night is still young and he looks through his phone to find another one of his young girl's.

CHAPTER 17

Na-jay & Fat-kat

K at you sure this the house Na-jay asks Fat-kat while he sits in the passenger seat of Fat-kat srt-8 jeep watching AJ house, yeah this the house I remember it and I logged into my phone Fat-kat replied, well we been sitting here all day and neither AJ or his bitch showed up yet I say we just break into the house and look for the money and drug's Na-jay say na you trippin I'm not no b-n-e type nigga I'm a home-invasion tie you and your bitch up tell me where the money at? type of nigga Fat-kat say na nobody said this was gonna be easy and you said you ain't want the lil bruh on this duty to watch the house Fat-kat say hell no we use the lil bruh to watch something before an you see what happen? Na-jay replies, I guess we just gotta wait then Fat-kat says, not for long because in the next hour I'm going home to my girl she keep texting and calling me asking when I'm coming home shit she might have something nice for me Na-jay tells Fat-kat Na-jay you always thinking with your dick but ight another hour and we gone Fat-kat replies.

911 CALL

911 what is your emergency? the 911-operator ask over the other end of the phone oh my god it's a dead body laying on the side of the road on the said of the graveyard a female tells the 911-operator, hold on miss the operator say you said it's a dead body laying on the side of the graveyard? how do you know this person is dead? the 911-operator

asks bitch because he's not moving the female say miss miss slow down I'm sending a police car and ems to you right now which block are you on miss? the 911-operator asks 10st and Woodland the female replies, ok miss help is on the way but please stay on the line until the police get their the 911-operator say what? the female asks miss I said stay there until the police and ems get their the operator says, hell no the female yells into the because if I stay here the police gonna want me to give a statement, fuck you I did enough by calling I'm not about to have my name in no paperwork, the female says while ending and taking off running

PETE, SHOOTER & TY

Shooter try Young phone one more time Ty tells Shooter, man I been calling his phone all day long why don't one of y'all try from y'all phones Shooter replied I called his mother phone and she said she ain't see him after he left the house this morning Pete tell's both Ty, and Shooter while he drives the stolen caravan through 9th st and 14th ave heading toward South Orange ave yo Shooter ain't that the dude Bark on the corner of the Ave? Ty asks yeah that's him yo Pete once the light turn green I'm a air son ass out Shooter say come on shooter we just got this van Pete replied, so what fool this shit stolen we could always get another one shooter tells Pete, alright just make sure you kill him because if you miss we shooting the fair one for getting the van hot Pete replied, whatever fool when the light change to green just pull up on him Shooter say go head Pete the light changed Ty tell's Pete, once the passenger window rolls down shooter stick his head out ayo Bark Shooter yells out the window who that? Bark replied it's Shooter Shooter says while letting off some shots boc, boc, boc, boc Bark takes off running down South Orange ave but he doesn't make it far without getting shot in the ass, go, go Ty yells from the back of the van, I think I got him shooter says to both Pete and Ty, I sure do hope so Pete says taking off straight down 9th street heading toward Central Ave so they could jump on 280 hwy because you saying your name before you started shooting was dumb is hell Pete tells Shooter, man that was some gangster shit Shooter replies while sitting back in his seat.

AJ, KRAZY J & BH

That food was good is hell, AJ how you know about that food spot all the way in Maplewood Krazy J asks J Maplewood is right next to Irvington and Newark it ain't like we left the state AJ tells his lil brother as he unlocks the doors to the black machine, so all three of them could get inside the car, AJ what time you gotta go pick up big bruh tomorrow? BH asks 9 in the morning why? AJ replied because it's already 9:30 at night BH replied damn I ain't know it was that late AJ saty starting the car, BH where you want me to drop you off at? AJ asks BH while looking at all the voice messages on his iphone 6, take me to my baby mother house BH replied which one? because you know you got two baby mother's bad Tina and Judy Krazy J say yo stop playing with me J for real, BH say yo hold on Tommy left me mad voice message I'm about to call him back AJ says while dialing Tommy number and placing the phone on speaker.

CHAPTER 18

Tommy & Big-dawg

This lil bruh calling me now Tommy says to Big-dawg while answering the phone, bruh what it do? Tommy asks AJ you already know the shit big bruh, I just check my phone and you left me some bad messages my bad but I been running around the city you know my bigger bruh come home tomorrow AJ replied, AJ look we need to talk asap but it can't be over the phone come to the lot on 1&9 Tommy tells AJ, alright I'm about to drop BH off and me and my lil brother will be their in a half an hour, AJ replied alright I'll be here waiting Tommy says while ending the call.

KRAZY J AJ & BH

Yo big bruh what happen? Krazy J ask AJ we about to go find out right after we drop BH off, BH we'll be there in the morning to pick you up before we go get big bruh from that hell hole AJ says while heading toward BH baby mother Judy house, that's cool with me BH replied while he rolled up his last joint of weed for the night.

LOCATION 1&9 CAR-LOT BEST WAY

AJ what took you so long? Tommy asks AJ as AJ gets out the black machine along with his brother, bruh we had to drop BH off at his baby mother house we here now so what's good? AJ says and Big-dawg what's good? AJ asks Big-dawg, same ole same ole Big-dawg replied Krazy J just stands to the side not speaking to either of the man toomy or Big-dawg in Krazy J book these two man are not friends they are just business partner's nothing more nothing less, AJ dig my people's on the inside told me who was the rat inside your set, Tommy says and then looks to Krazy J who still stands their like any minute he was ready to pull out his gun and shoot Tommy and his cousin down, who is it? AJ asks my people told me his first name is rome and he goes by Banger Tommy say AJ turns and look to his brother and shakes his head AJ can't believe what he just heard because he just saw Banger earlier today, and he had a funny feeling when he saw him, bruh if this nigga don't got no-paper work on the homie don't believe that shit what he saying, Krazy J tells AJ, Tommy shakes his head at what Krazy J just said because here he is tryna save both AJ and Krazy J from going to jail for along bid, AJ Big-dawg says taking over the meeting the dude Banger is also wearing a camera in his hat and his phone is tap me or my cousin don't know this man Banger never met him, so we have know reason to lie on him we tryna save y'all that's it, when our people hit us tomorrow he's gonna let us know all that they have on y'all and anyone else that this dude selling out, AJ just be safe and if you could take care of that dude so we could continue on doing business Tommy tells AJ ending their meeting.

AJ & KRAZY J

Big bruh you believe them? Krazy J asks AJ as AJ pulls into the parking spot of the hotel on 1&9 hwy where they gonna be staying for the night, lil bruh they have no reason to lie on him, AJ replied yeah that's true, so what we gonna do about BH? Krazy J ask lil bruh we gotta stay away from him until we know all they have on us from Banger, and being as Banger right under BH and BH deals direct with him if anything he got the most shit on BH, AJ say big bruh you think BH would rat us out? Krazy J asks bruh you never know AJ replied, why we ain't just stay at your house? you think they bug the house? Krazy J questions AJ nah lil bruh the house should be good, Kim text me and told me she was staying at her parents house for afew days so it ain't know reason to go to the house, AJ tells Krazy J, all big bruh you soft but sometime I wish I had a wife to go home to Krazy J says looking sad, lil bruh come on AJ says while exiting the car and j it's somebody for everybody you'll find love soon AJ say I hope so big bruh I hope so Krazy J says real low walking to him and his brother hotel room.

CHAPTER 19

Na-jay & Fat-kat

K at make sure you take it in the house the night is over Na-jay tells Fat-kat as Fat-kat pulls in front of Na-jay house on Hawthorne Ave bruh that's what I'm about to do ain't nothing out right now but police and robbers Fat-kat replied ight love you bruh Na-jay tells Fat-kat while he gets out the jeep, I love you more, go head I'm not gonna pull off until you in the door so hurry up before the police pull up Fat-kat replied that's why you my brother you always got my back Na-jay says closing the passenger door.

NA-JAY & TAE-TAE
Boy I thought you were never gonna come home tonight Tae-tae says, well you thought wrong Na-jay replied, well did you eat already? Tae-tae ask bay you know I was with Fat-kat so you know I ate already Na-jay tells Tae-tae, well go wash your ass and come get in the bed Tae-tae replied while making her way to their bedroom, ight Na-jay says rushing to the shower thinking Tae-tae wanted to have sex tonight but the only thing Tae-tae wanted was to know if Na-jay or his homie's had something to do with her cousin Rain getting killed, and it was that time of the month for Tae-tae so sex was not happening tonight …

BH

Yo Judy stop playing and open the door BH say BH has been knocking on his baby moms house door for damn near a hour and she still haven't answer the door, hey sweetheart the old lady says sticking her head out her house front door, what's good grandma? BH asks her Judy and that baby of her's left earlier the old lady next door says, they left? BH asks yes they had a lot of bag's with them like they were moving out the old lady say and how do you know they left with a lot of bag's BH question the old lady because I watch everything out of my widow's the old lady replied, alright thank you grandma BH tells the old lady and walks off, damn I knew I should had let AJ wait till I got in the house but where the fuck this bitch take my daughter? BH says to himself while thinking about the long walk he's about to make to home-base BH damn can't call nobody because my phone is dead, fuck BH says out loud …

DET. JACKSON & DET. KILLBURG

This is the second murder this weekend Det.Jackson says to his partner, Det.Killburg just shakes his head but to him it doesn't really matter it's blacks killing blacks long as they don't touch no white man or woman they could keep killing each other, did they i'd this one yet Det.Killburg asks ready to get on with the night, yeah they i'd him as Keith davis he had his i'd in his back pocket he lives on handing him her cell phone, Chadwick we already sent a patrol car to go notify his mother or father or who-ever he lived with at the address on the i'd Det.Jackson replied, alright let's roll then let the coroner handle the rest Det.Killburg tells his partner, Det.Killburg the Lt wants either of you, the white lady police officer tells Det. Killburgs while handing them her cell phone, Det.Jackson grab's the phone yeah Lt, Det. Jackson is this you the Lt asked yeah it's me Lt well I have bad news for you, Det.Jackson heart drop's due to him thinking they found out he gave Banger up, what's the news Det.Jackson ask voice real shakey, well after you two leave their I need you both at UMD,N.J a young black male has been shot in the ass, I need you guy's to go see if you could get a statement from him about what happen or see if he know who shot him, Det.Jackson heart slows down, ok Lt we're on it Det. Jackson replied before ending the phone call, Det.Jackson hands the white police office her phone back and tell her thanks and turns to his partner, what did the Lt want now? Det. Killburg asked, he wants us to go to UMD,N.J to try an get a statement from a young male who has been shot in the ass, Det.Jackson said well what are we waiting for Det.Killburg asked walking off to their unmarked police car, Det. Jackson looks to the sky it's gonna be along night he says to himself.

CHAPTER 20

Jabb

Big bruh where you at? Jabb asked Banger, I took it in the for the night why what's good lil bruh? Banger replied while laying in the bed with tt, nah it's nothing much I just wanted to let you know me, Kk, Pop-off, and Lucky about to ride out for the home girl I just wanted to keep you intune about it Jabb says, ight lil bruh y'all be safe Banger replied, we are big bruh love you Jabb says, love you more lil bruh, Banger feels like shit after hanging up the call with Jabb, because he had to give the police Jabb name also due to him being on the camera talking about a murder the Lt and the Det.'s wanted to know who he was and Banger gave him up lil bruh or not everybody had to go down in Banger book's long as it kept him outta going to prison.

KIM & MS. PAT

Girl where you been at all day? Kim mother Ms.Pat asked as soon as Kim walked through the front door ma me and Toya went to the mall if that's ok with you Kim replied, well did you eat? yes mother I ate, ok I'm just asking but lil AJ and your father already sleep, I was waiting up for you to get in the house Ms.Pat tells Kim, thanks ma but I'm tired and ready to go to bed Kim replied, ok sweetheart oh did you ever talk to AJ yet? Ms.Pat question Kim yes ma I told him I'll be home next sunday and that I needed some space apart and we have to talk and no I didn't tell him about the baby ma, but I promise to tell him sunday when I get home now I'm going up to my room ma good night Kim tells her mother and walks off to her old bedroom, good night to you too baby girl Ms.Pat replies.

BH & BEAR

Bear what's poppin lil bruh? BH what it do smokey? Bear replied what you just call me? BH asked nah nothing big bruh Bear says and goes into their set handshake, I see the police left the block BH says, yeah they just left I heard from one of my people's that somebody found a body on 10th st and Woodland, so that's where all the police at right now Bear tells BH, a Bear did you see bad-Tina today BH asked, yeah she home Bear replied, ight I'll see you later BH tells Bear and stepping off toward bad-Tina house, a big bruh, Bear yells to BH what's good lil bruh? BH asked stopping his walk, never mind bruh Bear say lil bruh you trippin BH tells Bear while continuing on his way to bad-Tina house, nah you the one who tripping Bear says to himself you smoking crack with that bitch, Bear wanted to question BH about it but he told himself at the last minute he'll just tell AJ and let him investigate the situation.

CHAPTER 21

D-low

Ma open the door D-low tells his mother from the other side of the front door, boy where are your damn keys? D-low mother asked him opening the front door, I think I left them in my room D-low replied back walking pass his mother to his small bedroom, I see you ain't bring none of them lil fast ass girl you always be with home tonight, what are they all on punishment? D-low mother yells to him, ma I'm not beat right now good-night D-low replied well good night to your punk ass to and you keep playing with them young girl's somebody gonna kill ya ass ...

BLACK

Cuz-o what's good with you? Black asked his cousin Baby while stood on 18ᵗʰ st and 18ᵗʰ ave corner in front of the poppy store, you know the shit lil cuz what's good? Baby replied, look I'm tryna switch my hood I'm not gonna beat around with the shit Black say why do you wanna do that? Baby asked man Na-jay and Fat-kat knock one of the lil bruh's off for next to nothing because he thought one of them tp nigga's was about to pop it off on him, so the young boy let go first and hit one of their home girl's, yeah that's some bull shit, but I been telling you lil cuz to switch now you see that phantom shit not for you, so look you about to get them round's under 118 and I'm a throw you some juice so you could bring ya lil bruh's with you if you want, damn Baby we family you really gonna make me get my round's that's

79

some bull shit Black says, look dawg everybody got their round's if you switch this what it is Baby replied, alright bruh let's just get it over with black tells his cousin, ight go over their and tell the lil bruh's that's in front of the red house I said give you yo shit baby tells Black, damn cuz you not gonna make sure they don't cheat me out my round's? Black asked look Black right now you on some hoe shit you switching or not? Baby asked yeah Black replied, ight go handle your business it's getting late and I'm about to take it in the house Baby tells Black, you said the red house right Black asked looking over at the red house where it's no less than 30 homies female's and dude's standing at, yeah now hurry up Baby says, ight Black says while stepping off toward the red house.

VICKIE

Yes bitch I called that nigga wife phone the other day and told his wife when she was finish with AJ to send him to my house, Vickie say bitch you are crazy Vickie friend Hazel tells Vickie over the other end of the phone, no bitch he crazy if he think he could just fuck me whenever he wants and call whenever he feels like it, he got another thing coming trust and believe that Vickie says, girl you know you my people's but you need to slow down and if what they say about AJ and his brother in the street's true they don't play no games Hazel tells Vickie, I don't play no games either I stay with my 380 on me Vickie replied Vickie you crazy and speaking of crazy you better hope AJ don't send his lil brother Krazy J to kill your ass Hazel say girl trust me when I tell you I'm not worried about AJ his wife or his crazy brother because I could get crazy right with they ass Vickie replied back meaning every word, Hazel girl it's late so I'll call you in the A.M, alright Vickie and be safe Hazel replied, oh I'm a be safe long as my 380 keep working Vickie replied, girl you shot out Vickie and ends the call, it's been a long night Vickie tells herself taken her dress off and getting ready for bath …

DET. JACKSON & DET. KILLBURG

I'm a just drop you off home because it looks like you to tried for anything else and I'll sign you off the clock when I get to the station Det.Killburg tells Det.Jackson, thanks Killburg Det.Jackson replied, hey what are partner's for Det.Killburg replied back, I knew we were wasting our time going to get a statement from that young kid who was shot in the ass Det.Jackson tells his partner, yeah I kind of knew that was gonna happen these so called street gangster's got that bull shit code of honor, but you and I both know that code only goes until they are facing time in prison and they start thinking about other guy's running up in their girl's then they tell everything Det.Killburg say your right on that one Det.Jackson replied back but make sure you come get me in the morning my car don't come out the shop till next week Det.Jackson says, that's no problem how's 9:30 am for you? Det.Killburg asked, that's alright by me Det.Jackson replied alright that settles it Det.Killburg replied.

CHAPTER 22

Old man

Y'all hold it down I'll be out in a few more hours the Old man tells all his lil homies under his set, and some of the few people he called friend's big bro hold it down once you out their and send some pic's of them bad bitches out their big bro the homie JJ tells the old man through the side of his cell door, I'm a send the mother load of everything through for y'all the old man says to all his comrades through the cell door, yo y'all gotta lower y'all voice's a male on the cell block yells out, yo who the fuck you think you talking to the old man asked, man I'm talking to you and anybody else that's feels like I'm talking to them the male replied back, oh yeah well state ya name killer you so much of a gangster right? the old man asked by now the tier is now silent except for the old man voice and the other man, my name King-s and I rep that phantom life under big homie Na-jay, King-s tells the old man, oh yeah well I'm da don and few call me old man and I don't rep nothing I am tp and with that fuck you, fuck Na-jay, and fuck that phantom shit, and you and all ya homie's can suck my dick and I'm not saying this because I max out tomorrow my lil homies would see you tomorrow so don't check in and I'll see Na-jay on the street's him and that fat bitch Fat-kat he always with, ight we'll see King-s replied but King- s truly didn't want any problems because he knew them tp nigga put on in and out the jail's, but he knows he can't try to peace it up now while everybody is listening on the cell doors because if he did he'll lose all respect and respect means a lot in the prison system, y'all hear this lil nigga the old man asks to anyone who would answer back to him, what AJ and no one else knows is the old man knows all that goes on in any jail in the united states and he also knows all that's going on, in the street's, if more then one person knows about anything then you could count on the old man finding out no matter the situation from who a home boy girl fucking to who shot who, the old man calls finding out information the owl game, because the old wise owl outlived all the other animal in the wild, lil nigga you'll be in icu before I touch some pussy tomorrow and as you and everyone else knows I'm that nigga and I'll be in some body girl a hour after I walk out them gates, so on that note tp the fuck up I'm going to bed the old man says as he turns around in his cell to get in his bed, for the last time and his roommate Sam is sitting on the top bed shaking his head, what now Sam? old man asked why you do that to that lil boy? Sam asked, shit it's one thing them phantom bitch's will learn they are old enough to be in prison they are old enough to get touched now leave me alone Sam I'm going to bed, the old man replied ok but just be safe out their Rich, Sam tells the old man, Sam is the only man allowed in this prison to call the old man by his first name, Sam go to bed the old man tells him closing his eyes …

T-DUB

What the fuck am I gonna do T-dub asked himself walking around in circles in his one bedroom apartment on 5th ave and 6th st on the Northside of Newark, fuck I know they gonna tell Lu, T-dub says while he grabs three more e-pills and pop them making it now 6 e-pills all together he took, I know what I'm a do T-dub says to himself while grabbing his high point 9mm from under the bed and letting himself out the front door.

PETE, SHOOTER,& TY

Ty hurry up Shooter whispers to him from outside of the srt-8 charger that Ty is inside of looking for the key to so they could steal the sport car, man I can't find the key Ty replied, oh shit come on Ty, Shooter yells taking off running back to the caravan that Pete sit's in waiting for them, Ty jumps out the srt-8 charger right as another West Orange cop car hit the corner, fuck Ty yells out loud as he jumps thru the open back sliding door of the van, gogogo Shooter yells, the chase is now on, Pete is trying his best to shake the police but the van is no match for the two police charger's behind them, slow down Pete the 280 hwy entrance coming up on the left Shooter say, I got it Pete replied while making the left turn just in time, damn bruh they still behind us Ty say I know bruh Pete replied doing the dash in the van which is only 120 mph Pete tries his best to get away dipping threw car's going around bends all gas but nothing is working for him, bruh I can't lose them Pete says out loud, bruh just take your time Ty tells Pete while looking behind them at the police car that's on their bumper, shit that was a state trooper that just jump in the chase Ty tells Pete, Pete is not scare, he never been in a situation like this before they just shot somebody outta the van a couple hours ago and they still have the gun with them inside the van, and they also have the gun they did the shooting with the other day in the van, so that's a attempted murder charge an a murder charge and now a eluding from the police and attempt to seal the srt-8 charger and the stolen van they are in which is a light charge compared to the other charge's, Pete slow up you know we gotta make a left or right 280 about to end Ty tells Pete but Pete mind is somewhere else and before you know it they are at the end of 280 hwy at first street, Pete bust a right turn we gonna bail out in the zone Shooter tells Pete, Pete is so scared that he tries to take the turn at full speed, that was the worstest thing he could have done the van slides straight going through a empty-lot then crashing into the wall which knock's them all out cold inside the van, this is office Seals to headquarters the suspect's have lost control of the stolen van and crash on First st in Newark N.J, suspect's are still inside the van I think we need EMT here asap, ok office Seals do you have your back up with you? West Orange headquarters asked yes and we are about to approach the van now, ok office Seals and proceed with caution, copy that! ...

CHAPTER 23

Jabb, Kk Pop-off, Lucky

Lucky yo drop me off Jabb says, for what bruh we riding out all night till we catch one of them fool's Pop-off tells Jabb, man drop me off to we ain't gonna find them punk's and we been riding all night long and the only people on their block's are lil homies and I'm not about to waste my bullet's on them Kk tells Pop-off, I say we just kill anyone of them lil nigga's because lil homies grow up to be big homie's one day Lucky say while driving down 19th ave towards 17th st yo Lucky ain't that's the dude Fat-kat srt-8 jeep right their, Kk says yeah that's him Pop-off says but not really knowing if it was Fat-kat jeep or not he just wanted to shoot somebody tonight, look when he gets to 15th st stop sign pull along side the driver side and we gonna air his fat ass out Jabb tells Lucky, what about me I'm not gonna be able to get no shots off from my side of the car Pop-off say nigga hang out the sunroof Jabb tells him ight cool replied Pop-off …

FAT-KAT & SAV

Yeah Sav you and ya lil homie's need to start fucking with me and Na more Fat-kat tells his lil bruh Sav from East Orange N.J yeah kat we just might do that we tryna lock the city down and them pills and weed you been fronting me could help do it Sav replied, so dig Sav after this last blunt of sour I'm a drop you off I was already on my way in the house when you called me and I gotta pick Na up in the A.M Fat-kat tells Sav pulling up to the stop sign on 19th ave and 15th st that's cool I'm about ready to take it down also Sav says while turning to hand Fat-kat the blunt of rolled up weed they been smoking, oh shit kat look out Sav yells, bocbocboc boomboomboomboomboomboom, Fat-kat jeep runs into a park, Sav looks up from ducking down low when the shots first started to ring off, kat, kat Sav says tapping Fat-kat to see if he was still alive Kat damn I gotta get the fuck outta here Sav says to himself while opening the passenger door taking flight forgetting to call for help for Fat-kat, in Sav head Fat-kat is dead so calling for help is pointless, but what Sav also forgot was to grab his iphone off the charge in Fat-kat jeep ...

JABB, KK, POP-OFF & LUCKY

That's how you put that work in Jabb says to his comrades inside in the car now Lucky hurry up and get us to Kk house we'll leave the car on William an Grove St and let one of them fools think they lucked up and found a clean stolen car Jabb tells Lucky ight that sounds like a plan to me lucky replied while heading toward East Orange N.J ...

CHAPTER 24

monday morning 8:00am AJ & Krazy J

J wake up, J I'm up bruh I'm up Krazy J replied to his brother, lil bruh I got some new outfits in the trunk of the car go ahead and jump in the shower I'll get in after you AJ says, see AJ here you go again tryna be my father Krazy J says while getting out the bed, whatever J just go get in the shower lil bruh …

RAHWAY STATE PRISON 9:32 AM

Damn about time they let his bitch ass out Krazy J says to AJ lil bruh chill out with that shit and what I tell you the other day about disrespecting big bruh? AJ tells his brother, whatever bruh I'm sitting in the back seat because I don't trust him sitting behind me Krazy J says as he makes his way to the back seat, fuck y'all pussy as cop's y'all could all die slow the old man tells the co's who standing in front of the prison, yeah alright ass-hole you'll be back a co name white tells the old man, not before your mother is dead the old man replied back getting into the machine, yo AJ what's popping? the old man asked once he's fully inside the car, you know the shit AJ tells him and they go into their set hand shake, lil j what's good? the old man says to Krazy J, dawg my name Krazy J so stop tryna play me pussy Krazy J replied what? the old man say you heard me Krazy J tells him, yo chill chill AJ tells them both, you got that one lil nigga the old man say I know I got it Krazy J replied yo AJ one of these days it's gonna be me and your lil brother the old man tells AJ, big bruh you fam and I got mad love for you but if you think you shooting the fair one with my lil brother you tripping, so what y'all gonna jump me? the old man asked, you damn right we gonna jump you Krazy J tells the old man jumping into the conversation, well y'all pick a day and time so we could get it popping the old man tells both the brother's as AJ pulls out the prison parking lot ...

KIM

Baby girl wake up! yeah mommy get up lil AJ and Ms.Pat tells Kim, what do y'all want? Kim replied still half sleep, Imade breakfast so get yourself together your father is already at the table waiting to eat Ms.Pat tells Kim ma what time is it? Kim asked, it's 9:43 am so come on Ms.Pat says, yah mommy come on lil AJ adds, alright I'm up I'll be down in 5 minutes Kim tells them both, ok let's go lil AJ Ms.Pat tells her grandbaby grabbing him by his lil hand and leaving Kim to get ready, damn this lady gonna drive me krazy Kim tells herself checking her phone for any miss calls or text messages, Kim text's AJ back I love and miss you too, love your wife, Kim text's AJ back even know she's upset with AJ she still loves him ...

D-LOW

Hello hey baby gm what who this? D-low asked the caller on the other end of the phone, oh so now you don't know my voice Qyanazia asked D-low real upset because she been waiting all morning for the right time to call him, nah I don't know your voice so who the fuck is this? D-low asked again, it's Qyanazia, oh my bad baby girl I'm not really a morning person D-low tells her, it's ok D-low I understand but I was calling to ask can we please chill today I'm tired of being up in this house, let's go out to eat or do something Qyanazia tells D-low, the do something part is the only thing that caught D-low attention, you know what I'm a take you up on that offer how's 12 something this afternoon sound to you D-low asked, that's cool by me Qyanazia argeed what D-low don't know Qyanazia would had agreed to anytime long as she got a chance to chill with him, ight I'll pick you up at your house D-low tells her, ok I'll be ready Qyanazia replied cool I'll call when I'm in front of your house D-low says while ending the call …

CHAPTER 25

Na-jay & Tae-tae

Tae-tae turn the news on for me Na-jay tells Tae-tae, what's wrong with your hands? Tae-tae asked Na-jay with an attitude she could give, all night long Tae-tae has been tryna get information outta Na-jay about her cousin Rain murder but either Na-jay truly ain't know nothing about it or he was on Tae-tae game, damn what's your problem? Na-jay asked Tae-tae while reaching for the remote on the dresser to turn to the news, this is eyewitness news if you are now just tuning in it's been a man found dead in his jeep early this morning the jeep has been shot multiple time on the driver side, the news reports tells his viewer's, John can you turn the camera this way so our viewers can see the jeep the reporter tell the cameraman name Jimmy, oh shit Na-jay yells out loud once the camera man has a full view of the jeep which Na-jay knows is Fat-kat jeep due to the rim's that are on the jeep, as I stated before earlier a man by the name of Khalif page has been found dead inside his jeep the police still have no suspect's for the killing or any witnesses, to the killing, fuck Na-jay yells, what are you yelling about? Tae-tae asked Na-jay coming back into the room from the bathroom, somebody killed my fucking brother Na-jay yells at Tae-tae, who? Tae-tae asked lost while looking at the news which has changed to another spot in Newark on first street, hold on tae Na-jay tells her while sitting up in the bed now looking at the news, we are now reporting to our viewer's three man were in a high speed chase late last night with West Orange police this stolen van which has crash into this wall killing two of the passengers of the stolen caravan, with the driver surviving the crash and now in police custody at UMD,N.J the names of the dead passager's are Tyquan, Goldsmith and Shad, Tyson and the surviving suspect is Pete Wilson, these are sad times in Newark, N.J our prayers go out to all the families who lost a love one this week, damn Na-jay yells cutting the tv off fuck my lil nigga's dead and my brother dead fuck, Tae-tae just stands to the side and watch Na-jay and says to herself good for you and all your homie's because in Tae-tae heart she knows one of them killed her cousin Rain …

DET. JACKSON & DET. KILLBURG

Well partner I guess killing people is never gonna go outta style Det. Killburg tells Det.Jackson, I guess not Det.Jackson replied, well let's get outta here they all ready bag all the evidences up so let's go Det. Killburg say ring, ring hello! yes Det.Jackson this is John at major crimes unit you won't believe what I found on the gun's that them kids had in that stolen caravan that ended with two of the suspect's dying, remember the killing of that girl that happen on 20th ave? and that shooting that happened on South Orange ave? John asked yeah I remember Det.Jackson replied well the gun's that were founded in the van were the same gun's that were used in both incident's John say hey John your the best Det.Jackson tells him, well Det.Jackson have a safe day out their John replied you to Det.Jackson say who was that? Det.Killburg asked as soon as Det.Jackson hung up the phone, come on we going to UMD,N.J I'll fill you in on it on the way Det.Jackson tells his partner …

VICKIE

Hello? hey AJ where you at? who this? AJ replied oh so we playing this game again? man who the fuck is this? I'm busy AJ says, nigga you stay busy, but this is Vickie, who? bitch don't ever call my phone again you play to many games, calling my wife and shit bitch when I see you I'm a knock you the fuck out AJ tells her yeah whatever nigga see me when you see me Vickie says before ending the call, that nigga really got me fuck up but I'm a show him Vickie tells herself as she strolls through her phone stopping on her cop friend number sending him a text telling him to hit her asap ...

BANGER

Tt good looking for the breakfast you the best baby girl, Banger tells her, yeah whatever Banger you say that but you still haven't made me wifey yet? Tt replied baby girl we good the way we are you damn near wifey all my shit here and I be here damn near every night Banger say you right Banger but my feeling just get in the way sometimes Tt tells him it's ok baby girl Banger tells tt standing up giving her a kiss on the lip's ...

SAV

Lil bruh I'm telling you shit got real last night I even forgot my phone in big bruh jeep I hope they just think it's his and don't go through it and learn it's my phone I ain't got time to be in no interview room or for them locking me up for his body Sav tells his lil bruh kick, as they walk to the store in their hood in East Orange oh Sav what kind of car you said it was? kick asked it was a blue gs-450 Sav replied like that one right their kick asked Sav while pointing to the park car, yeah just like that one, matter a fact lil bruh let's walk pass that car and see if the shit stolen Sav says ...

CHAPTER 26

BH

Yoo what's good? krazy where y'all at? BH asked Krazy J, man we sitting in front of old man girl house waiting for him to come out Krazy J replied real upset about sitting in front of the house waiting, yo I told y'all I wanted to go with y'all to pick him up BH say well take that up with AJ I'm about to give him the phone, because you acting like this my car Krazy J tells BH before handing the phone to his brother, yo what's good BH? AJ asked once he's on the phone, bruh I thought you were gonna come and get me before y'all went and pick big bruh up from prison? BH asked yo my bad bruh I forgot AJ tells BH lying AJ just really didn't want to be around BH due to all that's going on, and after he updated the old man on the situation he also didn't want to be around BH, and they agreed it'll be smart to stay away from BH, yo come and get me I'm at bad-Tina house BH tells AJ, you where? I remember dropping you off at your baby mother house last night AJ say man she wasn't home but that's another story I'm a be in front of bad Tina house so hurry up BH say and ends the call, so you gonna go get him? Krazy J asked from the back seat, yeah I'm a go get him we need him with us anyway? because soon as the old man comes out the house we going to holla at them bean and rice eatting mother fuckers, AJ tells Krazy J well here comes big bruh now Krazy J says while leaning back in the seat ...

JUDY & LADY

I can't thank you enough Lady for letting me and Alecia come stay with you I really needed to get away from BH and Newark Judy say I know how it can be no disrespect but I'm bless to not have any kids or baby father's that's just to much for me, Lady tells Judy who you telling? Judy replied mommy can we live here with Lady? Alecia asked her mother while coming in the house from the back yard, Alecia we, but before Judy could finish saying anything lady tells Alecia yes y'all can stay I would love for y'all to stay Alecia lady say thank you Ms. Lady lil Alecia replied and takes off running back to the back yard to finish playing, Lady you ain't have to Judy say I know I ain't have to but I love you and Alicia and I would hate for something, to happen to y'all Lady say thank you Judy tells her best friend while breaking down crying her eyes out …

BEAR & BANGER

What's popping Banger? Bear say you know the shit Bear what's good? Banger asked same shit yo look we having a surprise cook-out for big bruh you know he just got outta jail today Bear say what big bruh? who you talking about? Banger asked acting like he ain't know who who Bear was talking about, but he already knew from BH telling him a while back that the old man was coming home this month, the old man fool the only big brh we got other then AJ Bear replied, ight I'm a come through what time? Banger asked nigga we putting it together right now, and bring all your lil homie's or tell them to find a way we having it on home-base Bear say aight I'll be their Banger says and ends the call, I got him to say who the big bruh's were under the hood on the phone so I know I could get him to talk a lil more reckless Banger tells himself while starting his car …

JABB & TAE-TAE

So I'm saying Tae-tae we having a cookout and we having a lil get together for your cousin today on home-base so why don't you come thru and chill with me Jabb tells her, alright that's sound like a plan to me and Jabb thank you Tae-tae tells him, what are you thanking me for? Jabb replied you already know Tae-tae replied girl you playing games I'll see you on home-base Jabb tells her, alright bye Tae-tae says and ends the call, man she can't know about last night Jabb tells himself, Jabb why you looking like that? Lucky asked oh nothing y'all get ready the cab should be here in a minute Jabb tells his home boyz …

CHAPTER 27

Black & Baby & Na-jay

Cuz'o this fool Na-jay keep calling my phone Black tells his cousin baby, well answer it what you scared of the nigga? Baby asked what I'm about to answer it now black replied what? Black says into the phone what? Na-jay replied yo Black I need to talk to you asap you need to call a meeting they killed Fat-kat last night Na-jay tells black, so what you telling me they killed Fat-kat like I care they should of killed you to Black replied, yo Black you tripping where you at? Na-jay asked man fuck you and that phantom shit Black tells Na-jay what? Na-jay asked you heard me fuck you and that phantom shit 118 the fuck up Black says while ending the call, what the fuck is going on Na-jay asked himself as he grabs his key to his car and his mac-11 from under the bed, nigga's wanna play it's on I don't need nobody I'm a one man army Na-jay tells himself, what he say? Baby asked Black, what could he say? Black replied ight lil cuz I see you tryna be ya own man now Baby tells Black …

TOMMY & BIG-DAWG

Tommy Newark about to be on fire for a minute a dude just got killed on 19th ave and all these shootings going on throughout the city I hope the fed's don't start coming around Big-dawg tells Tommy, ight fuck it let's head to atl for a minute I need to see my kids anyway you wanna fly or drive? Tommy asked we driving right now so change highways and drive the turnpike all the way out Big-dawg replied, ight we out Tommy say.

V-NASTY

And where you think you going? V-nasty asked Qyanazia, ma why must I keep telling you I'm grown now Qyanazia replied, you gonna have to keep reminding me that as long as you living in my house and not paying any bill's, ms I'm grown V-nasty replied, Qyanazia can I come with you? Qwae-ma asked nah lil momma I don't think my man would be ok with that Qyanazia repliedya man Bar-man says jumping into the conversation, yeah my man and mind your business please Qyanazia tell him, well I just have one thing to say V-nasty husband Kintahe says while standing in the doorway to the living room, first I wanna say stop bringing all these difference guy's to the house and if you are having sex with these guy's please use protection because for one no one in this house is tryna watch no body kids amen to that V-nasty says from her seat, beep, beep look that's my bae I gotta go Qyanazia tells her house hold feeling like they all just team up on her, but at the same time putting on a kool-aid smile walking out the door to her so call bae car, let's me see how he look Qwae-ma says as she makes her way to the window in the living room, while looking out the window Qwae-ma get the shocking of her life Qyanazia bae is none other then D-low, D-low is sitting in his Audi with all the windows down oh my goes Qwae-ma says out loud oh ya god what? V-nasty asked nothing ma Qwae-ma says and walks to her room, Bar-man watches his twin reaction and takes a look out the window himself but his timing is a lil off Qyanazia and her bea are already pulling off ...

RAHWAY STATE PRISON

Sam we gotta move out on the dude King-s, big bruh left order's for us to do so, JJ tells old man sam, I hear you JJ but that boy is scared he haven't been out his cell all day that tells you right their and his homie's some punk's because they acting like they don't know what's going on, sam tells JJ, I eat all that old head but once a call is made we gotta handle any an all situation's JJ replied I understand young blood so y'all just go handle y'all business just don't kill the kid Sam say I can't promise you nothin Sam JJ tells Sam and walks away heading toward King-s cell.

CHAPTER 28

Det.Killburg & Det.Jackson

Pete you know you are in some deep shit, them gun's you got caught with has a murder an a shooting on them, so I'm a tell you like this help me help you Det.Killburg tells Pete, Pete moves his head from side to side thinking everything over, man fuck that Pete tells himself, ight I don't really know much but I could tell y'all about some murderers and where you could find some gun's at, Pete tells both the Det.'s Det.Jackson looks at Pete and just wanna slap the shit outta him, where is the loyalty at now a day's guy's snitching before they even make it to the police station now well my partner has a tape recorder on him, I gotta take this call real quick handle him Jackson, Det.Killburg tells his partner stepping in the hall way of the hospital, Vickie what? you know I'm at work, why are you crying Vickie? who hit you? what's his name? AJ? where is he from? home-base? alright I'm a handle it I'm a kill that mother fucker for hitting you Det.Killburg tells his black female friend Vickie before ending their call, damn I can't tell my partner about this Det.Killburg tells himself because to Det.Jackson Det.Killburg never been with a black women before, AJ and Det.Killburg beef just became personal now …

OLD MAN AJ & KRAZY J

Bruh BH gonna be mad we ain't come get him AJ tells the old man, he'll be alright the plod man replied while driving the black machine through North Newark toward lu block, look at it like this we saving our-selves and BH because if them pig's watching him they gonna be following us, an if we get into some gangster shit while we over here the police gonna see everything the old man tells AJ, you right big bruh AJ replied, there goes my mans Lu right their the old man says, Lu a Lu the old man yells out the open driver window, lu takes a hard look at the car and sees his old time friend old man, poppy Lu says as he approaches the driver side of the car, Lu what's popping the old man asked lu while popping the five with Lu, you know my friend are these ya two lil brother's AJ and Krazy J? Lu asked yeah these are my brother's the old man replied, but Lu I got a block meeting to get to where is your lil cousin at so we could handle this lil situation and I almost forgot to tell you your lil cousin not only switch from my hood but he also ran off with a 100,bricks of dope the old man tells Lu, oh poppy I didn't know nothing about no dope, my lil cousin ain't tell me that you know I don't get down like that Lu tells the old man yeah I know that's not your style the old man agreed with Lu I'm a call my lil cousin right now, yo time to get T out of the building Lu tells one of the poppy's who is outside watching his back, ok the fat poppy replied, so this is the famous AJ and Krazy J I heard so much about ...

T-DUB

Yo t poppy lu wants you out-side tim tells T-dub, what does he want? T-dub asked not really to beat to go see what Lu wants, I don't know poppy but he told me to come an get you tim replied and walks off to go back outside, what the fuck does this guy want T-dub asked himself leaving out the building ...

AJ, KRAZY J, OLD MAN & LU

Lu you seem like a cool dude AJ tells him from the passenger seat AJ Krazy J and the old man haven't got out the car yet they find it's know need to, oh there goes my lil cousin t come here Lu yells.

T-DUB

Oh shit they really came through, what am I gonna do now, did they tell Lu yet that I ran off with them bricks if not I still got a chance T-dub tells himself while pulling out his gun and shooting at the car even while lu is standing on the driver side, boom, boom, boom, boom, boom ...

CHAPTER 29

AJ, Old-man Krazy J & lu

Lil cousin what are you doing? those were the last word's Lu spoke due to one of T-dub bullet's hitting him in the head, go, go, go, AJ yells at the old man the black machine takes straight off with not one bullet touching the car, yogo back around the block I'm about to kill that fool Krazy J yells real upset that this is the second time he's been shot at by a poppy, nah we gonna catch him lil bruh he just shot his own cousin dumb ass the old man says as he takes a right turn doing damn near 50mph the black machine gets sideways outta control but the old man bring the car back under control with ease.

T-DUB

Poppy please don't die on me come on poppy get up T-dub tells a lifeless body, poppy he's gone tim tells him, they killed him T-dub tells tim, tim shakes his head no-no poppy you killed him tim says while pulling out his 357 revolver and put two bullet's in T-dub face.

KIM, TOYA

Girl when are you gonna call your man and go back home? Toya question Kim girl we gonna make up but for right now we need time apart Kim replied I understand girl but don't lose your man to these thot's out here Toya tells Kim, I know I'm not because I know what I have and I'll be damn if I lose my man, husband, baby daddy to any of these thot's Kim tells Toya, mommy when can I see my daddy?, lil

AJ runs up to Kim and ask you'll see your daddy soon go back and finish playing because we not about to be in this park all day Kim tells her son ok mommy lil AJ says and runs off to finish playing, see Kim that boy miss his father Toya tells Kim I know Toya I know, Kim replied …

TAE-TAE

Thanks ma for letting me move back in with you Tae-tae tells her mother, now stop it Tae-tae I'm your mother my house doors will always be open to you I just wish you would had left that good for nothing man Na-jay alone along time ago, Tae-tae mother tells her, I know ma I know but ma they having some type of get together for Rain on her block can I old the prix, I promise to put gas in it Tae-tae say girl go head Tae-tae mother tells her while handing her the car keys, thanks ma Tae-tae says while heading toward the front door, Tae-tae you be safe out their in them street's Tae-tae mother tells her, I know ma I love you Tae-tae yells to her mother going out the front door making her way to her mother grand prix …

BAR-MAN & QWAE-MA

So you telling me that's the same guy that tried to talk to you and disrespected you the other day that Qyanazia just got into the car with? Bar-man asked his twin Qwae-ma bar for the fifth time yes Qwae-ma replied damn what are we gonna do? Bar-man asked I don't know but let's just pray that AJ and Krazy J don't run into him while Qyanazia is with him, Qwae-ma say.

CHAPTER 30

JJ rahway state prison

Yo look at this fool he reading the qur'an now JJ says to his homie's JJ come on man I ain't mean to disrespect y'all last night.

BANGER, BH, BEAR,

Yo what time big bruh coming through we already got the food going on Bear says, man them fool's suppose to been came through here they were suppose to come get me before they went to north Newark, I guess they went without me BH tells Bear they went to north Newark for what? Banger asked tryna get some information outta BH, so he could have some shit for the camera other then him just having a good time at a block party, man some poppy and Krazy J had a lil shoot out the other day around second ave BH tells Banger, word? what was it over? Banger asked AJ fronted a 100 bricks to the dude T-dub he used to be tp but his pussy ass switch to that poppy nation shit so when Krazy J and AJ saw him while they were on their way to drop the 3,000 brick's off they just got from the connect, Krazy J asked asked AJ can he bust the dude T-dub ass you know like I know Krazy J always tryna catch a body, so anyway? AJ let Krazy J out to handle his business, but it ain't go how they thought it was gonna go, when Krazy J ran down oh the dude busting the other poppy's that were out their, started bust at Krazy J BH tells Banger, damn that's real Banger replied, while thinking as long as I stay around BH I could find out anything that's going on an it'll all be on candy camera …

JABB, KK, POP-OFF, LUCKY,

Bruh the block lit Pop-off says as he exit the cab on home-base, after paying the cab driver Jabb steps out last and looks around the area for Tae-tae, damn she ain't get here yet? Jabb says to himself, oh big bruh! Banger let me kick it with you Jabb yells to Banger …

JJ RAHWAY STATE PRISON

Y'all were beating down, I swear on my kids JJ I wasn't king-s started to say something but JJ cut him off, King-s, hold I'm not about to call you know King-s look it's kind of to late for all that the call has been made, eat this nigga JJ says as he backs out the cell and let his tp homie's rush King-S stabbing and punching on him, help, help, co help me please, somebody help me, King-S yells out as loud as he could tryna get some body to help him.

CHAPTER 31

Na-jay, & Sav

RIP Kat told me about you but, it's fuck up we gotta meet like this Na-jay tells Sav, yeah I know big bruh it was hard to get your number but I did get it Sav replied, I be knowing but you sure oh girl right about seeing them lil dude lucky park that car? in front of her house? Na-jay questioned Sav big bruh if molly said she saw them she saw them she knows it was him because he's friends with another lil tp dude name Kk and molly used to talk to Kk matter a fact Kk lives around the corner from here, Sav tells Na-jay oh yeah well let's go pay him a lil visit at his house Na-jay replied he's not their Sav say how do you know that? Na-jay asked because molly said she saw Kk, Lucky, and two other dude's she don't know get into a cab earlier, Sav say damn molly knows a lot Na-jay replied yeah she do big bruh Sav replied well look Sav ride with me I got word they having some type of block together on their block, let's go see if they out there and if you recognize the lil dude Kk due to him see him before let me know an I'm a hit his lil ass up with this mac 11, I got right here Na-jay tells Sav while showing him the gun an also drive Na-jay says an throws Sav the keys to a Audi s-8, but big bruh if the police get behind us I ain't really got the wheel, Sav tells Na-jay, well I got some shit for the police to now let's ride Na-jay tells Sav ...

D-LOW & QYANAZIA

D-low why you stop right here on this block, Qyanazia asked looking around, we good I just wanna talk D-low tells her while rolling up the tinted windows, so the inside of the car could be dark and nobody could see inside, we could of went to any place to talk why park on 18th st, an 19th ave? Qyanazia asked we good what you know somebody around here and don't want them to see you? D-low asked know not at all, Qyanazia tells him but is really lying she just don't wanna run into her brother's because this is their area.

OLD MAN AJ, & KRAZY J

Baby you know you more then welcome to come through the block for the get together AJ got the homie's and home girl's from all the way out west coming through, you and all your lil bruh's come through the old man tells baby, ight I'm a do that baby replied an steps off to go let his lil bruh know they all been invited to the old man get together, oh shit, oh shit, Krazy J yells as they drive thru 18th st yo go back around the block I just saw that fool D-low car and his daytime running lights are on so I know he's inside the car, word where he at? AJ asked turning around in his seat to look behind them, yo y'all chill out, what he do? the old man asked he disrespected our lil baby sister Krazy J tells him, oh word well look I'm about to bust this right at the light then I'm a bust another right on 19th st I'm a park, an you could cut through the side of one of these house's and bang his ass up, the old man tells Krazy J, yo j let me do it AJ says nah big bruh I got him he disrespected Qwae-ma I'm a kill him Krazy J replied ight just don't fuck it up AJ tells his lil brother while hoping he handle this job right, ight I'm a park right here make it quick an don't miss, and as soon as you get back in I'm a bust this left at the stop sign and we going straight to the block, y'all cool with that plan? the old man asked the brother's yeah they both replied at the same time, well Krazy J go handle your business the old man tells him.

CHAPTER 32

D-low & Qyanazia

I do truly like you but im not tryna have sex with you in your car Qyanazia tells D-low, why not? no one can see through my window we good lil momma, I'm telling you D-low say as he tries to give Qyanazia another kiss, no D-low stop Qyanazia tells him, what you green to having sex? D-low asks her tryna play mind games with her, yeah but before Qyanazia could finish saying anything shots ring out, boom, boom, boom, boom, boom, boom, boom, click, click damn shit jammed Krazy J says to himself and takes off running back through the side of the house he came from …

AJ, OLD, MAN, & KRAZY J,
You handle it the right way AJ asked Krazy J as Krazy J jeeped into the back seat of the car, yeah I handle it but it was somebody in the passenger so I off them to Krazy J replied with his heart beating fast due to the rush he just got from killing D-low and whoever was in the car with him, that's what I'm talking about the old man says while he sticks to the getaway plan and makes a left at the stop sign like they ain't just commit a murder, welcome home me the old man yells out loud inside the car gassed up to be apart of a murder his first day outta prison …

PETE, DET.KILLBURG, & DET. JACKSON
Well Pete you did the right thing, now let me and my partner get outta here and we'll come to the county jail to see you Det.Killburg tells

Pete, what? Pete yells why I gotta go to jail for? Pete asked, I told you both about three murder's an where you could find gun's and maybe even drug's, I told y'all all the info I know about my set phantom, why I gotta go to jail for? Pete asked Pete understand this is how it works later today me and my partner gonna go to the prosecutor office, an play the tape for her, then we gonna go to a judge to get a warrant for this Na-jay Smith and Frank love and all the other people under your organization that you gave us this information about, once all the information check out true we'll come to the jail like my partner told you an the prosecutor might wanna come to see you at the jail also but after all that we'll have you outta their do you understand that? Det.Jackson say yes I understand but could I have your card's Pete asked sounding real sad that he still was going to jail even after he snitched on all his so called homies, yeah you could have my card Det.Jackson tells him while handing him his card and leaving outta the room before he slap the shit outta Pete, what's wrong with him? Pete asked Det.Killburg, once Det.Jackson left the room, I don't think he likes snitches Det.Killburg tells Pete right before he leaves the hospital room also to catch up with his partner, man fuck the both of y'all and what y'all think, it's better them nigga's I told on then me, fuck that Pete tells himself …

YOUNG MOTHER MS.CAT

I want justice for my baby, he never hurt nobody, he didn't deserve to be killed and left on the side of the road like he was some type of dead animal, now I gotta bury my baby next week Ms.Cat yells into the phone at the prosecutor, Ms.Davis we are doing all we could do to find your son killer or killer's as soon as we find out anything I myself will update you, prosecutor ralph replied alright you do that Ms.Cat says while ending the phone call so what they say? Ms.Cat sister Max asked, he said he would updated me if they find out anything Ms.Cat replied ok let's pray they get caught one of Ms.Cat family member's says an all the family member's at Ms.Cat house for the over past for young Keith death agreed …

CHAPTER 33

Banger,& Jabb

So y'all the ones that killed Fat-kat last night? Banger asked Jabb for the second time yeah bruh Lucky was the driver and Kk, me, and Pop-off did the shooting Jabb tells Banger again, ight that's what's up you keep it up I'm a move you up to Lt Banger tells Jabb, but in Banger's heart he knows the only place Jabb is gonna be moving is to the county jail from the street's, a Tae-tae, Tae-tae Jabb yells to her, a big bruh that's Rain cousin I'm feeling her I want you to meet her she about to come over here now Jabb tells Banger what Rain? Banger asked the home-girl that got killed Jabb tells him while thinking Banger might be high because he keep wanting me to tell him something he already know, oh that Rain ight Banger replied …

DET. KILLBURG & DET. JACKSON

Partner that was just the Lt he said it's been another killing an it's on 19th ave an 18th st and it's also been another murder around second ave in north Newark, Det.Jackson tells his partner, I bet you the one on 19th ave is from them tp guy's Det.Killburg replied I don't think so let's just go to the one in north Newark because what the Lt said it was a male and a female that got killed on 19th ave while sitting inside a park car, so a boyfriend might of caught his girl cheating and killed her and her lover, the two killing's in north Newark are two poppy's Det.Jackson tells his partner, jack I just got a feeling this is from either them 118-guy's or AJ and his crew, so we're going through first, Det.

Killburg tells his partner while driving their unmark car toward 19th ave an 18th st, I think your right Det.Jackson tells Det.Killburg, but he hopes not because he promise his son Tommy he'll fall back from tryna lock up AJ due to their business relationship …

OLD, MAN, AJ, & KRAZY J

That's what I'm talking about krazy the old man tells him gassing him up, yo chill out we don't want nobody finding out about that shit AJ tells the old man, let's go to the corner store so I could get some newport's Krazy J says and all three of them walks to the poppy store on 20th ave an 21st before they make their way to where the action on the block is at …

SPECIAL CRIME UNIT NEWARK NEW JERSEY

Harris I think I founded something here? John tells Harris while standing in front of the dna system, what is it John? Harris asked some of the blood I founded in the back seat don't match to Khalif page, I ran a test on both, and I'm looking over it again and it don't match, hold John I got something also I got the phone unlocked, and this can't be Khalif page phone because from the picture's inside the phone is not of him not one of them, the only way this is Mr.Page phone is if he was gay, Harris tells John, well I'm about to text Det. Jackson and Det.Killburg and tell them to get down here asap John replied, alright do that and I'm a see if I could get any prints off this phone due to it being a touch screen an John try to but the blood into the dna system and see if you could pull up the person it belongs to, Harris tells John walking off to try an get a print off the phone …

NA-JAY & SAV

Sav open the sunroof Na-jay tells Sav, what for? Sav asked man just open the fucking sunroof Na-jay tells Sav ight Sav replied opening the sunroof, ight Sav as soon as you make the right off 21st, on 20th ave be on the look out for any one of them nigga's who you saw last night that killed Fat-kat Na-jay tells Sav, ight I got you bruh Sav replied …

111

CHAPTER 34

AJ, Old-man & Krazy J

J hurry up bruh we got the homie's waiting down the block to see me
the old man tells Krazy J, hold on with ya old ass Krazy J replied
grabbing his black bag with his items inside he just brought from the
poppy store ...

NA-JAY & SAV

Na that's him right their with the burgundy hat on, Sav tells Na-jay
lying, where? Na-jay asked looking around the block, standing by the
dude and that brown skin chick talking Sav says, what Na-jay don't
know is Sav just picked out any-body and the person he he just picked
out is none other than Banger, ight I'm about to pop it off, Na-jay says
while making his way out the sunroof of the s-8 ...

QWAE-MA & BAR-MAN

Qwae-ma try calling her again Bar-man tells his twin for the fourth
time, as soon as Bar-man questioned Qwae-ma on her movement
earlier today they been calling and texting Qyanazia phone to let
her know about the situation, hello? Qyanazia she picked up bar
Qwae-ma tells her twin, hello? who is this? the person on Qyanazia
phone asked who is this? your on my sister phone Qwae-ma replied
well miss this is officer andrew and I'm sad to tell you this but your
sister and her boyfriend has been murdered, officer andrew tells
Qwae-ma, Qwae-ma drops the phone, oh, my, god Qwae-ma says out

loud what happen? Bar-man asked looking at his twin then looking at the phone on the floor ...

JABB, BANGER & TAE-TAE

Tae-tae this is my big bruh Banger Jabb tells Tae-tae, how are you doing? Banger asked her I'm doing alright Tae-tae replied watch out somebody yells out loud Tae-tae turns her attention to the right where she heard the voice come from, what the fuck Tae-tae says as she and her boyfriend Na-jay lock eye's ...

CHAPTER 35

Na-jay & Sav

What the fuck is she doing out here Na-jay asked himself while pulling the trigger on the mac-11 boom, boom, boom, boom, boom, the first three shots hit Banger but the first shot Na-jay let loose hit Banger in the neck the second shot hit Banger in the heart killing him within seconds …

JABB TAE-TAE & BANGER

Oh shit Jabb yells while dropping to the ground behind a park car Tae-tae get down Jabb tells her but Tae-tae is in shock she can't believe that she just witness her boy friend come through the same block where her cousin got killed the other day and murder Jabb big bruh, Tae-tae Snaps outta it and drop's to the ground alongside Jabb behind the park car, now Tae-tae knows for a fact that either Na-jay had some-thing to do with her cousin Rain killed or he did it himself.

OLD, MAN, AJ, & KRAZY J

Oh shit you heard them shots Krazy J asks his brother and the old man as he takes off running out the store with the old man and AJ right behind him …

BH & BAD TINA

Hold Tina stop did you just hear them shots? BH asked bad Tina while she gives him blow job, yeah I eard them bad Tina replied

114

stopping but so what let me finish this off real quick bad-Tina tells BH grabbing his dick in a tight grip, I need some more of that fire crack you got bad Tina tells BH right before putting her mouth back on his dick, bitch get the fuck off me that's probably one of my homie's getting shot at, BH tells her while pushing her off him and fixing his pants and running to the front door, you could at least left me some crack to smoke you act like them so called homies care about you bad-Tina yells to BH, nah bitch you don't care about me BH replied back to her while going out the front door ...

DET. KILLBURG & DET. JACKSON

You heard them shots just now? Det.Killburg asked his partner, yeah I heard them Det.Jackson response running to their unmarked police car so he could hear where the shots going off at from the department on the police radio, Det.Jackson made it just in time for the call, shots fired location 20th ave an 22nd st possible homicide the lady at the department reports to all police officer's, let's go I know AJ and his crew did this shit also it's on their block Det.Killburg tells his partner, Det.Jackson just lowers his head I can't save him Tommy Det.Jackson says to himself, come on Jackson we gonna leave this scene to the other guy's it's nothing here like you said Det.Killburg says ...

LOCATION: ESSEX COUNTY JAIL ...

Yeah ma we good, nah he over their playing chess with the old heads on the pod, yeah he type good at it, AJ tells his an his brother mother V-nasty over the jailhouse payphone, alright ma love you too AJ replied before hanging up the pay phone feeling even more stress out then he was before he called his mother, the situation that AJ finds himself in is fucked up two months after Banger was murdered the police locked up AJ, Krazy J, BH, the lil homies Jabb, Lucky, Pop-off, an Kk the police were so upset about Banger getting killed, they rushed an put all the evidence they had from Banger camera an phone conversations together and got them all off the street's, the only two people that haven't been indicted that are apart of the inner circle of their set is the old man and Bear, their names are in the paperwork but they never really had know dealing with Banger so the police don't have anything on them, what has AJ so stressed out also is his wife Kim won't come to see him or let his mother bring his son to come see him, Kim also told AJ the news about the baby she was carrying but the last time they talked she claimed to had got an abortion, for Krazy J he tries to keep his mind on chess or anything else besides the street's or his family it fucked him up once he founded out that he killed his lil sister Qyanazia by a mistake when he shot up D-low car killing D-low also, one week V-nasty came to visit him and Krazy J told her the truth about what happened to his sister and from that day he haven't spoken to his mother not that she doesn't want to talk to him Krazy J just feels as he hurt his mother heart an he doesn't know how to go about fixing the situation so he just shuts his mother out his life for now.

JABB

Jabb sits in his cell hurting not only is he stress out over the many case's that he is fighting but he feels betrayed by Banger what he can't understand is how could Banger set not only the homie's up but also him Jabb loved Banger like he was his real brother it hurts that Banger turned out to be a snitch …

LOCATION 3-D-1 ESSEX COUNTY JAIL SAV & NA-JAY

Yeah Na I'm good just ready to get the fuck outta this county jail Sav tells Na-jay, yeah I know how that shit could be but yo they charged you with Fat-kat and young murder? Na-jay question Sav yeah bruh they just mad I ain't make no statement and they tryna scare me up, they also gave me some co-de's on Fat-kat murder, it's four of them Sav replied, word up? what's their names? Na-jay asked surprised by this info, remember what oh girl told us from my hood? Sav asked who? Na-jay asked, man the chick that saw that car parked Sav says while trying to speak in code's, oh yeah now I remember mollie or some shit right Na-jay asked remembering what Sav was talking about now, yeah, yeah they made them my co-de's lil dude Jabb, Kk, Pop-off, an lucky, they were in court with me the other day Sav tells him you were in court with them? I hope you got right with each one of them for killing bruh, Na-jay say nah big bruh I ain't move out on them I gotta stick with them for the matter of this case because if I fight them they might try to put everything on me, but once this shit over I'm a move out Sav replied I understand Na-jay tells him lying in Na-jay mind Sav must of had something to do with Fat-kat getting killed what else won't he move out on them fuck that case if you ain't do shit an the state don't have shit on him like he claim what's to worry about? Na-jay tells his-self ayo Sav lil Riq from the south on the pod with you right? Na-jay asked yeah he on the pod with me, oh yeah he told me you told him he had the building I been meaning to holla at you about that because he I don't think he should have that he to reckless Sav tells Na-jay kicking lil Riq back in, I told him he had the building call him to the phone Na-jay tells Sav, big bruh don't tell him what I told you ight Sav replied man call him to the phone Na-jay tells him getting more upset, hold on Sav replied, ayo lil Riq ayo lil Riq Sav tells out to get lil Riq attention, here he comes now bruh Sav tells Na-jay, yo who dis? lil Riq asked once he's on the pay phone, it's your father lil nigga Na-jay replies what? man who the fuck is this? lil Riq asked into the phone while looking around the pod for Sav slow down killa this na the one an only phantom life Na-jay say big bruh what's good? damn I heard what happened to kat I wish I was home so we could put it down for bruh him an young, then it's krazy how they put their bodies on Sav because he wanna make a statement lil Riq says talking fast, lil bruh where Sav at? he standing by you? Na-jay asked nah he walked off lil Riq replied while looking around for Sav, lil bruh I need you and the lil bruh's to pop Sav he the one that killed Fat-kat and young Na-jay lies about Sav killing young but he's truly unsure of who killed Fat-kat and he can't trust Sav word, so Sav has to go Na-jay tells himself, so handle that for me and I got that g status for you, I been hearing how you been holding shit down in their, I hope you ain't think I haven't been in-tune on what's going on in their, lil Riq is now gassed up and has a kool aid smile on because he always wanted the g, now it's being giving to him and the only thing in his way is Sav, I got you big bruh I'm a handle that shit tonight lil Riq replied one more thing lil bruh put the word out to pop any and all tp nigga's in their and I'm opening the book's back so bring home whoever you what get ya line deep you got that Na-jay tells lil Riq, I won't let you down big bruh I promise lil Riq replied right before he ended the call to rush and let the homie's know the news about his new found status that big bruh just pass to him, Na-jay sits the phone on the kitchen table and looks at the 3 females that are also sitting at the table with him, Erica, Lisa, and lady-red, these females, are the only people Na-jay keeps around him, the game has changed the dude's who suppose to be so called gangster's are telling at an all time high and they'll cross you for next to nothing, females are taken over the game and these women that are at this table right now showed their loyalty to Na-jay one to many times and they' are down for whatever Na-jay ask them to do, the love and loyalty they have for him has no limit's

DET. JACKSON & DET. KILLBURG

Hey Jack what's going on with you? I wasn't counting on you being in today Det.Killburg says to his partner, you know just because we got AJ and some of his crew off the street's don't mean our job is done, I'm tryna get all this stuff together so we could get the guy Na-jay off the street's next the da office checked out the kid Pete stories and they all add up so the da office want's all we have on Na-jay so they could start putting their case together Det.Jackson replies, so what about Pete is the da gonna let him walk away free from all the stuff they have against him? Det.Killburg asked, that's what they told me, but they wanna to put Pete back on the street's to work for them but Pete is against that so they giving him a 364 in the county Det. Jackson says, well I don't know why he didn't take the deal to work shit once Na-jay finds out he told on him he's good as dead from what from what I hear from the street's Na-jay is a loose cannon and now he picked up 3 females and they do whatever he tells them to do, Det.Killburg tells his partner, may I ask how do you know all this? Det.Jackson questions him, I have my source's Det. Killburg replies ending the subject right their, Det.Killburg still never told his partner about his dealings with Vickie even know they tell each other everything he just don't know how to tell Det.Jackson he got a thing for black hood rats

BEAR, OLD-MAN & TOMMY

What's good Tommy? What's good Bear? How's the brother Tommy replied you know same shit just tryna get to the money as always Bear says Tommy what it do? the old man asked You know the shit slow motion as always, how's everything with you? Tommy says man Tommy everything is on the up an up I called you here to home-base because I wanted to talk bigger business with you I just came back from kicking it with my homies out west and they gonna start blessing me I know you in on ya own wave but I'm now in place to make your and my situation better the old man says I hear what you saying bruh so what is it you got going on Tommy questions ight it's like this you and AJ been doing business for a lil minute bruh let me know he had mad love for you and also once AJ got bagged you still continued to flood us with the work when you didn't have to with that my homies out west giving me them birds for 11,500 and you and I know keys going for triple that now of days I know you got most of the city lock down and even many states and other city's you got on lock you with it? the old man asked Tommy stands their stuck he can't believe that the old man called him over here to offer him a partnership the crazy thing about it is Big-dawg told Tommy not to deal with the old man because he claimed he knew how the old man type's were they'll get their money and power up and they'll try to move in any and everybody pocket's but Tommy never thought the old man would want in on his movement, nah bruh I'm good my situation good where I'm at I can't just jump ship's on my people's after they been showing me so much love Tommy replied letting the old man know where he stands and also tryna get him to understand that no matter what good number's his homie's were giving him for the bird's he should be thankful for Tommy looking out for him, that's cool but I kind of knew you were gonna turn me down but dig take this bag it's 250 rack's inside I know I don't owe you know money for no work but this is just to let you know I appreciate you helping me get my army an money back right and if you ever are in need of anything let me know the old man tells Tommy know doubt bruh I'll hit you up Tommy says while sticking out his hand for a handshake to end their little meeting, ight much love the old man replies shaking Tommy hand while looking into Tommy eye's the look in Tommy eye's tells the old man that he's not ok with what just took place, the old man can read Tommy due to all the times he was in and outta jail he learned how to read people, ight Bear I'll holla at you Tommy tells Bear and walks off to his to his GL550 Benz which sits park idling in front of the burgundy trap house poach they are standing on.

BEAR & OLD-MAN

Big bruh Tommy wasn't feeling what you just came at him with Bear tells the old man I know lil bruh but I tried to bring him in on the movement I'm not about to sit up under no man when I can grow on my own and not for nothing I'm a boss of my own time I can't count on the next to feed me and mines Old-man replied yeah I understand that Bear that's why I offered to bring him in and AJ is away right now I'm back running this show and if I think something is better for us as a team that's what it is and AJ suppose to call me tonight I'm a let him know about what took place and what's to come because with this new work we getting a lot of people about to go broke because we about to lock cities and states down and who-ever not with us they against us the Old-man the way let's take this shit the fuck over from here to the west coast from the north-side to the south-side of the united states tp the fuck up Bear replies.

BH & JUDY

So how's your case looking? Are they gonna give you a bail so you can get outta their? Judy asked, man I don't really know to much right now the lawyer I got tryna do something but bring as I got all these charges I'm not about to get my hopes up to high but why you asking me about my bail like you really care if I make it outta here you still yet to tell me where the fuck you took my daughter to BH tells Judy getting upset, look Lee Judy says calling BH by his real name I don't have time to argue with you I'm putting Alecia on the phone now Judy replies Alecia come get the phone your father Lee wants you Judy yells to their daughter, here I come mommy lil Alecia yells back while running towards the bed-room Judy now shares with her old best friend lady who now is her full time girl friend now that they both agreed to be in a relationship hey daddy BH daughter

yells into the Iphone, hey baby girl I miss you BH replied, I miss you too, daddy I wanna see you Alicia tells BH I know you do but I'll see you soon daddy had to go away for a little while but your mommy gonna bring you to see me soon BH tells her, ok daddy but where you at? Alecia asked BH is stuck he doesn't know if he should tell his daughter the truth where he's at or not baby girl daddy is in school right now BH tells her, daddy I wanna go to school too, Alecia says, BH shakes his head because he knows his daughter wouldn't never wanna be in this place he labeled as school which is really the county jail, your mommy should be in rolling you into school soon BH replies, I know my mommy told me I get to go to a new school and I'm a have all new friends, BH is taken back by this news Judy never told him Alecia was going to a new school, a new school for what? BH asked himself why mommy sending you to a new school for? BH asked Because me and mommy moved away silly so I can't go to my old school no-more Alecia tells him moved away? What the fuck BH say what you say daddy? Alecia asked nothing baby girl, who y'all moved with? BH questions his daughter hoping to get an answer from her, we live at lady, mother fucker you think you slick Judy yells into the phone after snatching it away from Alecia Judy left the phone on speaker and ran to use the bathroom but she caught the last part when BH was questioning Aleica about who they lived with, bitch you really playing games with me moving my daughter away? This my word when I get outta here I'm a find you bitch an take my daughter away from your dumb ass BH tells her, nigga I hope your black ass never get outta their and make this your last time calling my phone Judy replied right before she ended the call.

BH

Damn this bitch moved my baby girl away from me fuck BH yells out loud standing up from his seat at the payphone BH you good? One of the little homie's under tp name Ju asked him, man get the fuck away from me BH tells him and walks off heading towards the gym to walk his stress off well fuck you to Ju replied under his breath.

JUDY & ALEICA

Mommy is daddy mad at us for moving away? Aleica asked no baby daddy just upset he's in school he'll be ok Judy replied lying Now go put some shoes on we gotta go meet lady to have lunch with her she's on her lunch break ok mommy Aleica replied.

KIM & TOYA

Kim you need to take that man son to see him keeping lil AJ away from him not only hurting AJ but it's also hurting y'all son Toya tells her best friend Kim as they eat their lunch at fridays on Rt 22 in Union N.J Toya I know it's just I'm so mad at him right now just after we made up and I forgave him after all that bull shit we were going through he goes to jail after I told him to leave the streets alone I know I'm suppose to stick by his side and all but I kept telling him I wanted him to stop running but he didn't listen and I feel like if I go running supporting him he's just gonna come home and think it's ok for him to jump back into the street's thinking I'm a be their for him again Kim replied Kim I can understand all that but that's your husband and you'll suppose to be their for him no-matter what Toya tells her, well look I'm a just go pop up on him next week visit but I'm not taken my son Kim says look Kim whatever you do I'm with you I just hope you make the right choice this time Toya says and what do you mean by that? Kim asked nothing at all Toya replies but is lying to Kim by Toya saying what she just said Kim knows she's talking about the abortion Kim just had done Kim and Toya been friends to long for either of them to try and slip in some slick words into one of their conversation's but Kim let it bypass and starts back eating her steak and butter potatoes.

BLACK & BABY

So look right this how shit about to go we gonna start getting them birds off the old man for the low which is gonna be 18,500 that gives us a lot of room to play with and we gonna give him pounds of this sour for 2,600 baby tells his little cousin Black as they sit inside the living room of baby one family house which he shares with his police chick shay, that sounds like a plan to me black agreed but whatever baby said black would had agreed to, but what you gonna do about the other offer that he gave you about all of us being tp? Black asked I'm not gonna lie little cuz I thought about it and I know I got my own hood but when you add it up we only so deep we in a few cities and states but it's nothing compared to how the level the Old-man and AJ got tp on with that we gonna have a meeting tonight and I'm a let all the homie's know that we about to switch over and any-body not with it they can roll out somewhere else baby say so what about the homies in other states? and what status he giving you? Black asked not really caring about the outta state homies but just really wanting to know if he was gonna be able to keep his g-status they coming through too but for the status he blessing me with is the double which is cool by me and yeah you could keep your g baby tells him Black is caught off guard because he tried to word it just right so baby wouldn't know that his status was all he was worried about, baby is no fool he knows that many home-boys only care about is status now a days, I guess what they say is true if you can't beat them join them Black says and starts laughing baby just sits there looking at Black not nothing saying, what bruh I said something wrong? Black asked, nigga I should slap the shit outta you, if you can't beat them join them I'll never fold I just know when something good comes my way to take it and with that it's about money to me now get your dumb ass out my house saying some dumb shit like that, and you better be on time at to the meeting it starts at 9:30 tonight have all your little who switching with because time is money Baby tells him, and leaves out the living-room let yourself out and make sure you lock that door behind you baby adds, man I'm tired of you talking to me like that black says real low so Baby can't hear him but you gonna see which black says as he lets himself out the front door …

PETE,& KI

Yeah Baby I'm good what these nigga's know what it is on my pod I'll do anyone of these nigga's in here or on the street Pete tells his girlfriend Ki whos from Avon ave and 11st bay don't be mad but I been hearing something on the street's and everybody saying you done and you never coming home Ki tells him, what who said that? Pete asked getting heated over what Ki just told him, just some hating as nigga's and bitch's but don't trip I put all them in their place Ki replied, it's ight I'll be home within a few weeks I'm getting a 364 I'm tryna get time serve Pete tells her, bay I looked your charge's up and you got some real charge's you don't gotta lie to me I'm not going no where if you gotta do some time I'm a ride Ki tells him meaning all of what she's telling him, nah they dismissing a lot of my shit just Pete tells her, alright bay the lady just knocked on the door so our time is up and when are they moving you to the max building so I could catch a ride with my cousin alicia down here I'm sick of getting on the bus with all them people Ki says, where is your cousin from Pete asked tryna do his homework on her cousin so he'll know what type of person his girl was gonna be around cousin or not, she from down bottom new community Ki replied, bay I'm about to come home soon so don't worry about getting a ride from her, what Pete haven't told Ki was he's on pc (protective-custody) the da office had the county jail place Pete on pc because they know if it gets out that he's telling the gangs inside the jail gonna kill him so Pete going to the max building won't be happening for Pete, bay go head before that lady come back tripping because you still here Pete tells Ki tryna rush Ki out the visit before she start to questions anything else, love you Ki tells him leaving out the visit room love you more Pete replies ...

QWAE-MA & BAR-MAN

Qwae-ma come on get up I'm sick of you just laying around all day it's starting to get played out now Bar-man tells his twin sister, Qwae-ma takes her head from under the sheet's and Bar-man can see she's been crying again bar man takes a seat on the bed Qwae-ma you crying not gonna bring her back I know that you might don't wanna hear it but she's gone to a better place so stop crying Bar-man tells her, Bar-man it's easy for you to say all that but if I wouldn't had never told AJ and j about that dude disrespecting me our sister would still be here Qwae-ma replied qwae it's not your fault you didn't know Qyanazia even knew him so stop blaming yourself now mommy said get up we got an air-plane to catch to Miami in 3-hours so hurry up Bar-man tells her and makes his way back to his room to finish getting ready for their getaway vacation nobody understands I need to talk to AJ and Krazy J next time they call because I know they can somewhat relate to what I'm going through they the ones who did it Qwae-ma says to herself now blaming her older brother's for killing their sister.

LOCATION ESSEX COUNTY JAIL KK, POP-OFF, LUCKY, 3-B-1

Ayo let me holla at y'all real quick Kk tells Pop-off an Lucky ending their beat-down that the two were in, as the three young man walk towards Kk cell a dozen set of eye's follow them lucky turns around an catches a couple people watching them man why the fuck everybody looking at us lucky says to Kk and Pop-off as they walk into the cell, who Pop-off asked turning around to exit the cell, nah chill pop Kk tells him stopping Pop-off in his tracks that's what I wanted to talk to y'all about my lil mans gravy he under that toe-tag set, who? Lucky asked and can't believe somebody calls their self gravy, yeah I know Kk says but my lil mans his name gravy he from underwood by 18th ave he on3-d-1 he sent me a kite telling me he overheard some lil dude name lil Riq in the gym talking about moving out on all tp nigga's

125

in the building Kk tells them hold lil Riq that's phantom? Pop-off asked yeah him he suppose to have the g now from what gravy put in the kite he sent over, so that's why all them nigga's were out their watching us walk to your cell? Lucky says, I guess so so be on point Kk tells them What? Be on point? I don't know about how y'all might feel about it but I'm not about to sit around and let thses nigga's move out on me I'm a Pop-off first Pop-off tells them, word up Kk it's just us three over here I'm not about to wait for these nigga's to build up the heart to move out on us we gonna move first lucky tells them, alright that settles it let's eat, you trust your man's gravy word right? Lucky asked, hell yeah that's bruh Kk replied ight let's eat then Pop-off says as they exit the cell.

LOCATION 3-D-1 LIL RIQ

Ight look lil Ray you dawg and troub pop Sav diggie you and Joey watch out for the police matter a fact pop Sav on the dance floor so everybody could see it and know we cleaning house of all fuck boyz and we bringing in all real nigga's lil Riq tells the few homie's that are inside his cell Riq so what about them tp nigga's dawg asked we gonna start moving out on them tomorrow you already know once y'all pop Sav they gonna lock the pod down for the rest of the day lil Riq replied attention all area's you have a code green 3-b-1 you have a code green on 3-b-1 the lady over the loudspeaker say fuck hurry up and pop that Sav now he's on the phone again lil Riq tells the homies who he picked for the job at hand, fuck who popped off on 3-b-1 It old them nigga's over their to wait till tomorrow to pop them tp nigga's I know no one ain't tryna disrespect my g-call lil Riq says to himself as he walks out his cell to watch lil Ray, Dawg and Troub eat Sav.

SAV

Yeah ma I love you to, yeah I'm ok I'm a call and check up on you tomorrow they just called a code so they might be about to lock us down if the code to outta control, most likely it's a fight, ma I'm good I'm not fighting Sav tells his mother, Sav lil Ray says to Sav while tapping him on his shoulder, what bruh I'm talking to my mother Sav tells lil Ray getting upset due to lil Ray disrespecting him by coming to talk to him while he's on the pay phone, yeah well tell that old bitch to sick my dick lil Ray said to Sav and popped off on him, with trob and dawg following up right behind him, lock in it's a code next door co Jones yells out loud to the tier, as co Jones walks from behind his desk that's when he notice a man being beating by three other man hey stop hey co Jones yells to the attackers trying to get them to stop beating the man they are jumping co Jones runs back behind his desk and picks up the phone to let central control know it was also a fight going on, on3-d-1 everybody lock in co Jones yells out again.

LOCATION 3-B-1 LUCKY, POP-OFF, KK

Nigga shut the fuck up Pop-off tells the one phantom dude he's beating up who's yelling for help, Kk is under the tv fighting two dude's they are trying their best to surround him but Kk is doing a good job of keeping them in front of him, for Lucky he's not so lucky right now it's three people he's fighting he's trying his best to kick up but he's no match for them so he just tries his best not to fall to the ground because he knows if the three guy's get him down they gonna stomp his light's out, Pop-off shows up just in time sneaking one of the three guy's that Lucky was fighting, let's get it Pop-off tells the dude as they go blow for blow everybody on the ground the turtles yells out loud to all the inmates who are either standing around watching the fight or who are involved in the fight.

JJ UNION COUNTY COURTHOUSE

Hey Mr. Jason Jackson I'm your public-defender I'm here to represent you on the matter of an assault charge that happened inside rahway state prison on a samad sweets the state is offering you a 5w/85 ran wild meaning it won't run with the time you're already doing, being as the man was stabbed multiple times the state can bring an attempted murder charge on you and not just an assault so what do you wanna do? the public-defender tells JJ while looking at the paperwork inside his hand JJ just sits there an look at the pd like he's some type of fool to think JJ was even gonna consider taken this deal the state is offering, first off Mr. whatever you name is JJ says to the pd oh I'm sorry my name is John Brady the public defender replied, well John first off I been in an outta this system all my life you coming back here telling me a 5w/85 like I'm supposed to take that deal then you jump to talking about some attempted murder tryna scare me up JJ tells the pd, know Mr.Jackson I'm not tryna scare you up the public-defender tells JJ, look just shut the fuck up and stop cutting me off I know the state don't have shit on me I also know sweets made a statement saying I stabbed him but I also know he took his statement back so look go out their and tell the da office to either run that shit with the time I'm already doing or they could suck my dick I max out in 4 days fuck I look like coping to a new bid now go head and tell them what I said before you make me madder than what I am JJ tells the pd who takes off out the back of the holding cell area, fuck wrong with that nigga JJ says out loud to himself, excuse me I'm not tryna be all up in your business but you said you max out in 4day's what do that mean you going home? A female voice asked JJ from the next holding cell over from him, yeah why? JJ replied, know I just wanted to know but how much time did you do? the female asked, I did 7 years but you sure do ask a lot of questions but what's your name ma? JJ asked my name is Zoe but I only asked you those questions because I overheard you talking to your lawyer and this my first time ever in jail and it's sound like you know about the law from the way you were talking to your lawyer Zoe say Yeah I know a little about the law but what are you locked up for? If you don't mind me asking JJ replied some drug's it was my ex-boyfriend stuff Zoe says damn well where he at? JJ asked he home he wasn't at the house when they raided the house Zoe tells him, I hope he popping you're bail or signing an affidavit to cut you loose JJ says he was suppose to do that 3 months ago but he always got an some bull shit excuse why he ain't do it yet, but fuck him Zoe says while breaking down crying, ma look I don't make promises to people and don't keep them, what's your last name because if everything go right today I'm a come pop you're bail what's your bail anyway JJ say my bail only 50,000 cash or bond Zoe replied JJ shakes his head damn her nigga left her in jail with her bail only 50,000c/b and she locked up for his shit an she ain't rat him out straight rider and she sounds good JJ thinks to himself but you don't gotta pay my bail you don't even know me Zoe tells JJ turning down his offer, Zoe is not about to let this unknown man get her hopes up high shit her own boyfriend or her family haven't even came to post her bail, why would this man do it? Zoe says to herself in Zoe book all real nigga's were either dead or in jail even know this guy was in jail Zoe only knew him for a few minutes so she couldn't stamp him as a real nigga, dig ma I'm a man of my word what's your last name? JJ asked again, my last name is Rollins Zoe tells JJ giving in to him and his promise, Mr.Jackson JJ lawyer says while walking into the back of the holding area, the state has agreed to run the charges together and for you coming back for sentencing this paper right here is an waiver for it due to you maxing out in four days so just sign here an here and you're be on you're way the pd tells JJ while looking at the floor, that's what I'm talking about JJ says while signing all the legal papers have a nice life Mr.Jackson the pd says to JJ taken the paperwork back and rushing away before JJ could respond back, I guess you're going home Zoe says sounding sad, little momma stop sounding sad I'm coming to get you JJ tells her meaning every word he told her, we'll see Zoe replied hoping that JJ truly came through so she could get outta the hell hole she's in what some people call the county jail.

3-HOURS LATER 5:45PM GOOBA, OLD-MAN & BEAR

Dig Gooba I know you and you're block heart homies been having 21st an 16th ave locked down for years so my offer of putting y'all on might don't sound like much but I'm offering you a spot at the round table with me and a couple other people the old man tells Gooba, alright I hear you so what do you got going on? Gooba asked my people's giving me them bird's for 21,000 racks the old man lies and I'll give you it for 21,700 I'm throwing you that price so I could re-up faster and you know them bird's going for more then that the old man tells Gooba trying to sell him the offer, ight I could fuck with that but is

129

the shit stepped on? Gooba say what Gooba means by stepped on is, have the bird's been cut already, nah it's straight off the boat the old man replies, ight bet I'm a let the bruh's know we gonna deal with you from now on, an with that I need you to bring me ten of them through tomorrow I'll have the buy money with me Gooba tells the old man, hold bruh I'm a front you the work the old man replies, bruh know disrespect but I don't do know handouts because I know nothing in life is free Gooba replied meaning every-word, that's what's up the old man says a little disappointed because he wanna to step in Gooba pocket by fronting him the birds Surr who the fuck is that? the old man says about the tinted 2010 srt-8 charger that just hit the corner side way's, Bear whips out his pistol to shoot at the car, nah bruh chill that's big head Shorty from 18th ave an 19th st Gooba tells them just as the stolen car pulls to a stop in front of the three man, what's happening with y'all fool's? Shorty says once the driver side window is down, nothing is good with us the only thing that just almost happened is us filling that car up with bullet holes Bear tells Shorty with murder in his eyes and on his mind, Bear and Shorty have been beefing for year's over a female that's been playing them both, man fuck you nigga Shorty replied, what I'll do you're car thief ass right now Bear says pointing his 17teen shot 9mm at the car, hold y'all nigga's chill out not on my block Gooba tells them both, yeah chill Bear the old man says agreeing with gobba, ayo Shorty how much you want for that car the old man asked this I want 3,500 being as it's an 2010 and it's type old Shorty replied what I'm not about to pay that much money for know stolen car the old man tells him, man we ain't gotta pay him shit I'll take that shit from him give me the word Bear say Nigga I wish you you would I'll murder your dumb ass Shorty tells Bear, hold, hold Bear chill out and Shorty you're not killing shit this way I'll body you myself if you touch my little bruh the old man tells him, yeah aight Shorty says and starts to let the car roll back off, yo chill Shorty look I'll give you an rack the most the old man tells him, ight you want it now Shorty replies ready to get out the car due to him getting chased all day by the state boys in the car, did anybody see you in it the old man questions because he knew if he did something in the car it would come back to Shorty if people knew he had the car, nah I got it by myself and know body knows I got it Shorty lying Shorty and his mans ron been smoking weed in the car most of the day, ight take this rack the old man says while going into his pocket to pay Shorty, yo Bear drive this over to my house the old man tells Bear after paying Shorty, ight yo this shit not car-jack? Bear asked Shorty while taking the gloves Shorty just had on so if the police ever got the car his prints won't be on it, nigga I don't car-jack Shorty replied lying, but for the srt-8 charger they were buying it wasn't car-jacked I got it from a car-wash in South Orange Shorty tells him, ight Bear replied getting behind the wheel of the car ayo Gooba I'll see you tonight the old man tells him while getting into his all white bmw m6 coupe, bet I'll be their Gooba replied stepping off down 21st with Shorty.

V-NASTY, KINTAHE, QWAE-MA, BAR-MAN

V I think you need to get Qwae-ma some professional help look at her sitting over their zoning out Kintahe says to his wife, V-nasty takes a hard look at Qwae-ma who sits on the right side of her in the other row on the airplane, Qwae-ma sits there looking spaced out, she'll be alright hopefully this trip to Miami will help her V-nasty replied well lets just hope so because I sure don't want that girl hurting herself Kintahe says while looking back over at Qwae-ma.

QWAE-MA

Damn big sis why did you have to get into that car with that guy, I feel as it's my fault that you're gone Qwae-ma says to herself in her head, Qwae-ma listen to me I'm in a better place now so stop stressing yourself it was my time to go it's not your fault it was god's plan for me so with that live your life I'll be on the other side waiting for you Qyanazia spirit tells Qwae-ma, what the fuck was that Qwae-ma says out loud Snapping outta her day dream catching a shock look from her family, know I'm ok she tells them, Qwae-ma are you alright? Bar-man asks oh it's nothing Qwae-ma replied not wanting to tell him

131

because she knows he'll think she's losing her mind but Qwae-ma knows what she just heard and she's gonna do what her big sister asked of her to do and live her life to the fullest starting with this trip.

TOMMY & BIG-DAWG 6:30PM

It took you long enough to get here Big-dawg says to Tommy as Tommy walks into their sneaker store located in jersey city N.J off hwy 440, man you know how rush hour is at this time everybody tryna move out for the weekend Tommy replied, yeah I know the shit but what happened with the old man Big-dawg asked while looking around to make sure no customer's could hear their conversation, man he offered me an partnership on some birds he's suppose to be getting for the low, Tommy tells Big-dawg with his face getting tight over the situation bruh I told you once he got right he was gonna try some fast shit didn't I? Big-dawg says once again but fuck all that what we gonna do about this shit because the numbers he's getting them for I know he's gonna try an lock down the city with the dope he's getting Tommy tells him, I see you got your mind set one way so with that we gonna pay somebody to kill him so we could keep our hand clean and outta the way Big-dawg replied, so who do you have in mind and how much you tryna pay out? Tommy asked I know the first person I have in mind you might don't agree with, Big-dawg says, man who is it? Tommy asked ready to just get on with the situation, I say we have your father do it, being as he's a cop he could kill the old man and say he thought he was reaching for a gun Big-dawg says Tommy like this is the best plan in the world, what? Are you outta your fucking mind? Tommy says a little to loud because all eyes are now on them from the few customers in the store, yo chill the fuck out Big-dawg tells Tommy while placing his arm around Tommy shoulder and walking him towards the back of the store where they keep all the stored sneakers at, bruh I only said you're father because you know the police can kill somebody and get away with it hands down but if you're not trying to involve your father that's understandable but know I'll never put pop's under the gun to go down for know shit like that, moving on doe it's a dude name Na-jay from the south side of

Newark, an from what I heard from my little mans him and AJ set beefing so we'll throw him 100,000 racks and let him kill the Old-man Big-dawg says that sounds like an plan Tommy agrees shaking his head up and down, alright that settles it I'll hit my little mans and tell him to let the dude Na-jay know we wanna meet him about some business and you never know we might could flood him with the dope being as we not dealing with AJ and them know more Big-dawg says, you right bruh but I just wish I could holla at AJ because I know little bruh ain't know about the Old-man switching whips up on me, and I still got love for AJ Tommy replies cousin you can count on it that AJ knew all about it AJ is the old man second in command with that fuck him to money don't stop it keeps going Big-dawg tells Tommy before walking off to ring up an custom man I know little bruh wouldn't go out on me like that Tommy says to himself but Tommy also knows people loyalty only goes so far now a days …

AJ & RICO

Big bruh visit day tomorrow you got wifey coming to see you? Rico asked nah little bruh me and her type going through something you know how that goes AJ replied I know the shit bruh but my girl cousin coming to see me tomorrow and I'm a bring you in on her cousin you could put her on you're list tonight so she could come see you Rico tells AJ, AJ sits and think it over for a minute fuck it what are the chances of Kim coming to visit tomorrow at the same time AJ says to himself ight we could that give her my name I'm about to go holla at Miss.Wells about putting her on my visit list, you got her name already? AJ says yeah her name Lexi Carr she from Woodbridge Rico replied that's cool but what's her address? AJ says you could put any address Rico replied ight call her and let her know and I'm a go handle Miss.Wells AJ says getting up from the table they were sitting at, ight I'm a do that now and tell you're second wifey Miss.Wells I love her Rico says playing yeah ight AJ replied big bruh you she's feeling you Rico tells AJ while walking towards the pay phones.

AJ & MISS.WELLS

Miss.Wells how are you doing? AJ asked the co as he walked up to the officer desk I'm doing alright what's good with you doe? Miss. Wells asked AJ looking him up and down letting him know she was feeling him everything good but I need you to put this name on my visit list so my little peoples could get in tomorrow AJ tells her, what's her name Miss.Wells asked taking out an pen from the front pocket of her shirt and an small notebook her name is Lexi Carr AJ tells her oh what's this one of you're thot's coming to see you? Miss.Wells ask nah it's just an friend AJ replied but he could see Miss.Wells ain't believe him, yeah whatever playa I'll do it for you now Miss.Wells tells AJ picking up the officer phone dismissing AJ out her face, AJ gets the message and turns and walks away but before he could get far Miss. Wells calls him back I knew I had to tell

something you're little homie's lucky and them got into a big fight on their pod, Miss.Wells tells him, my little homies I don't know what you're talking about I don't got no little homies AJ replied AJ just because I got this outfit on don't mean I don't know what's going on out in the world, I know who you are trust and believe that I'm from higher-court pj so don't let my job fool you, with that I was just updating you on you're people's Miss.Wells say ight good looking out AJ replies AJ thought's are all over the place what could have my young boy's got into? and this co bitch must really be feeling me to put her job on the line to tell me some shit like that, fuck I gotta set up an conference call with the homies I know somebody heard about what happened already, fuck I hope none of my young boys got hurt because if so I'm shaking this fucking jail AJ says to himself while looking around the pod for his little brother to let him know this news.

2 HOURS LATER 9:30 PM HOME-BASE

I'm happy everybody made it here on time for this meeting the old man says to all the homie's who showed up for the meeting that's taken place in-side the back of an trap-house on 20th ave I'm not about to keep y'all to long I'm a get right to it because we all going out tonight to celebrate because what's about to take place tonight calls for an celebration the old man tells all the gang member's, only people that knows about what's about to take place is Gooba his shot caller his homies that showed up the Old-man and Bear somewhat, what this meeting is about is all the 118 homies are falling under tp and I'm blessing baby with the double anyone disagrees with this? the old man asked, the tp homies are shock, but they all ok with the changes no says anything so the old man moves on to the next topic with that I'm moving AJ up to triple og and I'm making Bear an og and the last thing is from here on out we are united with the black hearts so give them the same love and respect that you'll give an tp homie anyone not feeling what I'm doing can get out the whip the old man tells anyone who doesn't like these changes again but like I stated before what this meeting calls for so we all going out tonight to all stars the realest nigga in the rap game coming through yo-gotti an we all know when real nigga's in the building bad-bitches gonna come be their also so all y'all nigga's go home and tightening up we'll all meet at white castle down the hill and if you gotta choppa bring it out tonight just in case something pop's off the old man tells all his little homie's the old and now the new ones, some of the homie's at the meeting start to think about not showing up to the club because they know with them being this deep going anywhere things are sure to Pop-off but they also know if they don't show up whenever they showed their face again thing's were gonna be real for them, but for the old man he's hoping something pop's off with who-ever just so he could test his new power with his new army.

MEANWHILE IN THE SOUTH SIDE OF NEWARK N.J

So you understand me? the dude has to go asap Big-dawg tells Na-jay I told you already I'm on it I'm a man of my word and with you already paying me all this cash up front what choice do I have but to come through on the hit if you got this much cash to place on the Old-man head I know you also got more cash to place on my head and I'm not looking for that kind of problem Na-jay replied filling

Big-dawg head up with a little bit of bull shit to Na-jay he wouldn't care if Big-dawg placed money on his head also because he wouldn't be the first person to do it, bruh we just need the job done and I promise you we'll throw you all the dope you want for the low Tommy tells Na-jay I got you I'm a send my lady Lisa and she's gonna rock him, Na-jay says what you gonna send a bitch at him? Tommy asked surprised who are you calling a bitch Lisa asked whipping out her 44 long revolver with Erica and Lady-red following up right beside her taken out their twin 45 pistols with extended clip Na-jay just stands there with an kool-aid smile on his face because he sees the scared look in Tommy eye's and also Big-dawg eye's who you callin a bitch? Lisa asked again, Tommy doesn't answer because he's still in shock that these women have his life in their hands, and the look in their eyes tells Tommy that they all have lost soul's, now y'all chill out Na-jay tells his baby girl's ending the little show they just put on, pardon me ma for the disrespect Tommy says now that the women put up their guns but like I was telling you I'm a send Lisa to work him and we should have the job done by next sunday Na-jay tells them, why so long Big-dawg questions Na-jay shakes his head look bruh hitting the old man not that easy he always has a lot of people around him and trust me they'll take a bullet for him and no one is not gonna be able to just walk up and take him out so that let me handle the job y'all paying me to do Na-jay say You right bruh you got our number's hit us Big-dawg says, and him and Tommy steps off walking down Hawthorne Ave, to their park cls63 benz bruh I hate people like them all that money they making and they won't get their hands dirty Erica says to Na-jay yeah I know baby girl but that's how the game goes hoe nigga's winning Na-jay replied while watching Tommy and Big-dawg walk down the block.

DET. JACKSON & DET. KILLBURG

No baby I don't think that's an good idea no my partner won't be You're won't what? Det.Jackson asked his partner while getting into the police car catching Det.Killburg off guard oh nothing really my lady friend wanted to know would you like to talk to her friend Det.

Killburg says with the iphone glued to his ear and his thought's hoping Det.Jackson said no, sure why not it's not like I'm married any more Det.Jackson replied fuck Det.Killburg says to himself, what he say? Vickie asked over the other end of the phone, he said yeah he'll talk to her Det.Killburg tells her, ok so you off work now so why don't y'all come take us out tonight Vickie says, I don't think that'll be a good idea Det.Killburg replied, what won't be an good idea? Det.Jackson asked pulling their police car into the police station parking lot so they could get their personal cars, they wanna go out tonight Det.Killburg lets his partner know, that's ok tell them we'll be their in an hour top's Det.Jackson say Vickie we'll be there in an hour Det.Killburg tells Vickie and ends the call real upset, so what's the girl name who's gonna be my date tonight? Det.Jackson asked her name Hazel Det.Killburg tells him, and what's you're girl name? Det.Jackson asked Vickie Det.Killburg replied alright Det.Jackson say with his thoughts going over the names, names that he knows black women to carry not an white girl that he's kind of sure of Det. Killburg hooked him with just now.

V-NASTY, QWAE-MA, BAR-MAN, KINTAHE

Baby I see you're enjoying yourself now V-nasty says to Qwae-ma yeah ma I'm feeling better now I really needed this trip thanks a lot ma Qwae-ma replied know baby you should thank your brother's when they call tomorrow because they the ones who paid for this trip V-nasty tells her, they did? an I wish I would had knew that I would had told them to just give me the money Bar-man says sitting from his spot at the buffet table, boy shut up and finish eating your food it's getting late and we have a lot of things set up for tomorrow Kintahe tells him, alright give me an minute let me finish these last two rib's Bar-man replied grabbing the rib's off his plate.

AJ & KRAZY J

Lil bruh what you about to use the bathroom? AJ asked his brother due to Krazy J putting up his bath towel over the cell room window, chill out I'm a show you Krazy J replied while fixing the window block, AJ just sit on the bottom bunk thinking why did I tell Miss. Wells to put him in my room, look what I got bruh Krazy J says while taking out an cell phone from the inside of his pants man where the fuck you get that from AJ asked standing up from the bed, the lil homie turn up on b-pod sent it over to me he went home tonight they just dismiss the body he was fighting Krazy J replied powering up the phone, man I hope he ain't give you no tap phone AJ says bruh lil bruh a stand up dude Krazy J replied yeah that's what BH said about Banger and look how shit turned out AJ say you right bruh but I'm using this shit tap or not fuck that Krazy J says holding the phone and taking a seat at the foot of the bottom bunk, matter a fact let me use that shit to call the old man I gotta see did he holla at Tommy AJ said disregarding all he just said, yeah I thought so Krazy J says while handing his brother the cell phone.

OLD-MAN & BEAR

Nikki I'll be home later on tonight, I know I promise not to stay out tonight, yeah I know you're gonna throw all my stuff out, ight love you, the Old-man tells his wife who he's been with for the pass 15yrs damn big bruh wifey on your ass to? man my bitch was tripping also when I told her I was going to all stars with the gang tonight Bear says, while sitting in the passenger seat of the old man white 2017 range rover sport, lil bruh that's because they know the thot's gonna be in the spot the old man replied while double parking the range rover in front of the night club and all the homies doing the same right behind him making a show of a soul train line of all the exotic car's big bruh we can't park here Bear tells him and why the fuck not? this my state now and I'll do as I please in my state the old man tells Bear putting the truck in park, man who the fuck is calling my phone now? the old man says while grabbing the ringing phone outta the cupholder, Bear shakes his head at the old man because he knows for one that it's gonna be some shit tonight because not only has the old man been drinking remy but he's also took 3 grams of mollies, who the fuck is this the old man asked yelling into the phone, nigga you better fix your tone when you're talking to me it's AJ nigga, AJ replies back into the phone, AJ what man who ever this is stop fucking playing on my phone the old man replied bruh this me you bugging AJ tells him before he could end the call, after catching the voice the second go round the old man knows it's truly his young boy AJ, oh shit lil bruh what's good? Ayo Bear AJ on the phone the old man tells Bear gassed up that he's talking to AJ due to AJ and them situation they haven't been talking to each other this is their first time talking each other without an third person, hold on I'm about to put you on speaker the old man tells AJ, yoo Bear says once the phone is on speaker, Bear what it do? AJ replied Bear what's goodie? my boy Krazy J says, yo AJ who that? Bear asked that's my brother fool I got y'all on speaker to AJ replied, man why y'all talking so low for? the old man asked nigga we on an cell phone and we're in jail have you forgot Krazy J tells the old man, oh shit my bad bruh damn it is kind of late I should have been caught on the Old-man replies Yo where y'all at Krazy J asked happy that he's talking to the bruh's, we about to step in all stars right now yo-gotti coming thru tonight the old man tells him, word damn I know them hoes gonna be in their Krazy J says yeah you know the shit Bear say ayo what happened with Tommy earlier I didn't call moms yet to see if you called and gave her the 411 AJ asks the old man ya mans turned me down the old man responded I told you he was but I'll hit him tomorrow and before AJ could say another word the old man cut him off man fuck that nigga the old man says nah bruh not that one he held me down AJ says you know what you right the old man replies but what's been going on AJ asked changing the subject man everything is on the up an up all the 188 nigga's now tp and we united with the black hearts, AJ and Krazy J look at each other shock by what they just heard, why they switch for? AJ asked I offered Baby the double and I offered Gooba a spot at the round table they both agreed the old man replied, and you got the triple now Bear tells AJ gassed up for AJ because he moved up, what? Triple? bruh I told you I ain't want that shit AJ yells into the phone at the Old-man forgetting all about him being in jail on an cell phone, AJ dig what's done is done but this y'all cell phone right? the one man asked while

139

checking his mirror's, yeah AJ responded real heated ight we only gonna be in here for about two hour's we gonna hit the phone back tonight when we leave here I know y'all wanna call some hoes so go head the old man tells AJ trying to get him off the phone now because he knows AJ is upset with the changes that were made and the old man wasn't in the mood for AJ bitching about it, ight tp Krazy J says into the phone AJ handed him back before laying down in his bed, us Bear and the old man says at the same time before ending the call.

KIM & TOYA @ ALL-STARS

Bitch I can't believe I let you talk me into wasting my money to come see some rapper who don't know or care about either one of us, Kim says what? Girl yo-gotti is a nigga and don't take it as we paid to come see him, take it as we paid to have an good time Toya replied, yeah whatever Kim say Kim don't look but it's a guy with long dreads with an true religion outfit on coming your way Toya tells her, what? Kim replied a little to late, damn ma I been looking for you, where you been at? the unknown man walks up beside her, Kim and say what? Do I know you? Kim asked yeah you don't remember me? the dread head asked trying to run some old school game on Kim which Kim never once in her life had used on her due to her being with AJ her whole life, nah I don't remember you Kim tells him while taking a deep look at the dread head to see if she really knew him, damn that's fucked up but my name Cash money you remember me now? Cash money asked not at all Kim says and turns away from him in her seat, damn ma it's like that? You really don't remember me? Cash money says still trying to run his game, look ma my crew is all out Cash tells her hoping telling her what crew he was with might win him some points with her, nah never heard of you or your crew Kim tells him lifting up her shot glass to take a drink of the remy she ordered, I heard of your crew Toya says jumping into the conversation oh you did Cash money asked Toya with his eyes still on Kim.

OLD-MAN VIP AREA

So what you tryna say ma a nigga can't take you home tonight the old man asked the 5'7 brown skin women with the amber rose hair cut, nah I don't even know you like that but we could exchange numbers and go from their, the women replied that's respectable what's your name again the old man asks her high outta his mind, my name is Lisa she tells him again ight Lisa what's you're phone number the old man asked while unlocking his phone to save Lisa number.

BEAR & BACK

Ayo you use to be phantom right? Bear asks Black as they walk toward the bar to try and grab up some women to take back to the vip area with the ones they brought in from standing in line outside, yeah I was Back replied, damn now this the third hood you were under Bear asked tryna play Black on the low, yeah something like that Black says not catching on but even if he did catch on to Bear dissing him he wouldn't of said nothing back to him about it, shit ain't about nothing nigga's switch everyday you tp now and ain't no switching from tp Bear tells him meaning every word, I know that shit bruh Black replies.

DET. JACKSON & DET. KILLBURG

I really let you guy's drag me out here to Union county to some damn night club in Elizabeth Det.Killburg says out loud as he stands in the long line waiting to get inside club all stars, bay chill out once we get inside and get some drinks in us things gonna be better Vickie tells him, while holding his arms, yeah Kill chill out we're turning up tonight Hazel tells Det.Killburg calling him by the nickname she gave him, you're alright baby Hazel asks Det.Jackson bayying him already, yeah I'm good just haven't been to an club in along time that's all Det.Jackson tells her while looking at all the double park cars in front of the night club.

V-NASTY & KINTAHE

See I told you that all my baby needed was a nice get away V-nasty tells her husband, you sure did bay Kintahe replied while laying on the other side of the bed, now all I gotta do is get through to J and let him know I still love him no matter what and we could get through what happened with Qyanazia together, V-nasty tells says, just give him time he'll come around Kintahe tells her while wrapping her in a tight hold in his arms.

ALL-STARS OLD-MAN, BABY & GOOBA

Ayo Baby ain't that Black and Bear over their all up in that dude face at the bar? the Old-man asked word up that is them Gooba replied pushing the light skin chick that was sitting on his lap off him, let's go see what the fuck is going on the Old man tells them and while making his way to the bar with his new founded army behind him, Lisa just sits at the table and wait to see the show she knows is about to happen because if what Na-jay told her is true then she'll be leaving this club in 10 minutes top.

BEAR, BLACK, KIM, TOYA, & CASH MONEY

Bruh I better never catch you in my big bruh wife face again Bear tells Cash while point his finger in Cash face, Bear it wasn't even like that you and your boy tripping over nothing Kim tells Bear word up Toya adds, we're not tripping this nigga was all up in your face Black says pointing at Cash, tryna get some points for standing up for AJ while he's away, man y'all nigga's got me fucked all the way up she ain't have a problem with me all up in her face so miss me with all that shit Cash tells them both, and tries to walk pass them so he could let his crew know it was about to go down, but before Cash got outta arm reach Black popped off on him stumbling Cash, oh y'all tripping Cash says throwing up his guard to get the fight started, yeah we tripping Bear says while busting a bud-ice bottle upside Cash head, y'all stop Kim yells.

OLD-MAN, BABY, & GOOBA
Oh it's going down the Old man yells to his crew and rushes to the bar.

TONE & DOLLAR
Ayo Tone ain't that Cash at the bar fighting Dollar asked standing up in the vip area of all stars looking toward the bar, where? Tone asked looking around then spotting Cash getting jumped by two dude's, oh shit that is him Tone says and then see's a group of nigga's running toward the fight also, yo let's go Tone says running towards the fight it's on Dollar yells to their crew in vip and they all follow behind Dollar and Tone to go help Cash.

KIM & TOYA
Girl let's get the fuck outta here Toya tells Kim pulling her by the arm trying to get Kim outta the club before shit got realer than it was, nooo we gotta stop them from from fighting Kim says pulling back from Toya so she could break up the fight, Kim are you fucking crazy let's go Toya tells her pleading with Kim as she notice two group's of people heading toward the fight and also security coming, Kim also see's this and comes to her senses.

DET. JACKSON, DET. KILLBURG, VICKIE & HAZEL
What the fuck, why everybody coming outta here like the building on fire? Det.Killburg asks while watching all the people coming outta the club running toward their car's or to the corner to call the people who brought them here or the cab's they caught to the club on the low, come on let's go black people all was fucking up an good thing Vickie says to the group of people she came to the club with, where we going? Det.Jackson asked not understanding what was happening, due to him in so long, bay it's over something going down in-side so with that we're outta here before they start shooting Hazel tells him, being as Det.Jackson and Det.Killburg were both off duty and outta their district and county it was nothing they could do to help this situation.

IN-SIDE ALL STARS

I'm getting too old for this shit the Old man says as he knocks out the second person who just ran up on him, yo baby watch out the old man yells to Baby just before a dude knocks him upside the head with an liquor bottle knocking him out cold, fuck the old man says to himself taking off towards Baby who lays on the floor out cold, get the fuck off me Black tells the security guard who holds him in an tight sleeper hold trying his best to put Black to sleep, shut the fuck up the guard tells him tighten up the hold, what the fuck? the security guard says due to Gooba stabbing him with his pocket knife, you heard what the fuck he said let him go Gooba tells him stabbing him again, I'm about to beat you're young ass Tone tells Bear ass they stand toe to toe ready to throw down.

ALL STARS PARKING LOT

Hold on Toya that's that bitch Vickie, Kim tells her friend and makes her way to Vickie is at, girl let's go we'll catch that bitch another time Toya replies, but Kim just keep her pace heading toward Vickie who's not even paying any attention to nothing around her.

AJ & KRAZY J

So we breaking day? Krazy J asked while checking out his facebook page on the iphone, yeah I'm a stay up and wait for the bruh's to call back or I'm a call them in another half-hour AJ replied bruh you good? Krazy J asked his brother, yeah I'm good AJ replied real dry Krazy J knows his brother is lying, AJ tried to call Kim multiple times and she haven't answered not one time or even called back yet, yo you gonna call your lawyer ty Krazy J asked his brother calling AJ lawyer by her nickname, yeah I'm a call as soon as day-break AJ replied.

KIM & VICKIE

Talk that shit you were talking over the phone that day now bitch, Kim says to Vickie who turns around and is shock to see who's standing behind her, what who are you? Vickie asked playing like she ain't know who Kim was Vickie been did her homework on Kim and checked out her facebook page to see how she looked just in case something like this ever happened I'm AJ wife Kim say, Hazel and the two Det.'s are shock to her this, it's truly an small world Det. Det. Jackson say to himself, oh you're Kim nice to meet you Hazel says trying to downplay any situation that was sure to happen inside the parking lot look bitch mind your business this is between me and this bitch Kim tells Hazel while sizing Hazel up just in case Hazel wanna any problems Miss Kim I'm a officer of the law so I myself am letting you know to let any situation you have with my lady friend go because I won't have any problem placing you in jail right beside AJ Det.Killburg tells her, Kim is surprised by this cop statement because she never once said AJ was locked up, so how does he know that information Kim ask herself looking at the white police officer, just as the thought hit her that either Vickie told the cop about AJ or they both had dealing with AJ being placing in jail, shots sound off bloc, bloc, bloc, bloc, bloc, everyone inside the parking lot drop's to the ground hoping not to get hit by an stray bullet, boom, boom, boom, boom, Det.Jackson police mode kicks in and he reaches for his police issued 40cal Pistol which is always on his hip but not tonight due to them going out to the club Det.Jackson left his gun at home because Vickie let them both know they weren't gonna be able to get inside the club with guns on them police or not, fuck let's get to the car Det. Jackson tells them and duck walks towards his G550 benz wagon.

HOME-BASE 2;30

Bear did you check on everybody that was with us the old man asked walking back into the trap house kitchen from using the bathroom, yeah I called Baby and them they good and Gooba was in the car with us so we know he made it home safe but some of the bro's phones going right to voicemail they phones might be dead Bear replies we'll just try them in the am but I'm about to call AJ and see if they still up I gotta let my boy know about his wife and also the shit we got into over her the old man tells Bear while pulling out his cell phone to call AJ.

ESSEX COUNTY JAIL LOCK-UP

Ayo worker that breakfast was cold is hell, next time make sure my shit hot Pop-off yells out his cell open food-port to the old head kitchen worker, who just keeps walking paying Pop-off know mind, ayo Pop-off leave that nigga alone before he do something to our food, Kk tells him Man that crack head mother fucker knows better to play with our food we tp he know the shit Pop-off replied, y'all nigga's gotta keep it down people trying to sleep y'all loud is hell troub yells out his port trying to start a problem with Pop-off being as he just heard Pop-off rep tp nigga who the fuck is you? Pop-off asked troub phantom life the one and only that's who the fuck I am troub tells him, oh yeah well fuck you and you're set Lucky yells out his port jumping into the conversation nigga fuck y'all Dawg yells out from his food port, it's now mayhem with each side disrespecting each other.

ESSEX COUNTY JAIL 3-C-3

So what you're telling us is Na-jay put the green light on all tp homie's AJ question Sav in-side the pod gym Yeah bruh like I don't know really why but I holla at him right before they tripped on me my so called homies Sav replies, what AJ doesn't know is Na-jay never told Sav it was a green light to eat any tp nigga's once Sav founded out that he was on the pod with AJ and Krazy J, he made it his business to holla at them, Sav just learned that Na-jay put the call out when AJ brought it up, but like if anything I'm not trying to deal with this phantomshit no more Na-jay just to much he be tripping Sav tells AJ, bruh what you think should we take him? AJ asked his little brother who stands to the right of him, I'm saying bruh if we going to war with Na-jay we might as well take him he could be useful I know he knows some type of information Krazy J replies not putting know cut on his words even know Sav is standing right in front of them, ight bruh we gonna bring you in under my brother AJ tells Sav and makes his way outta the gym leaving both Sav and Krazy J alone in their, so what now? Sav asked first off you gonna tell me where Na-jay live and we'll go from their Krazy J replies.

AJ 10:30 AM

After locking back into his cell AJ puts up the window block so he could use the cell phone, boom, boom yo AJ yells to whoever is knocking on his cell door while tucking the cell phone, big bruh they said they on their way now Rico tells AJ from the other side of the cell door, ight come get me when they call our names AJ replies taking the cell phone back outta his pants, I got you Rico replied, after cutting the phone on AJ tries to call Kim but her phone goes right to voicemail, fuck AJ says out loud to himself, AJ has been up all night after the old man told him what happened last night and that Kim was their with some dude, AJ couldn't sleep and has been calling Kim phone all night, the information Sav told AJ and the kite AJ got from the center runner about Lucky and them popping off on the phantom nigga's AJ doesn't even care about it his mind is on questioning Kim about this dude she was out at the club with and that's all.

LOCATION SOUTH ORANGE AVE & 8TH ST

I see you out the hospital, how you're ass feel Snap asked his cousin Bark trying to jail off Bark due to Bark getting shot in the ass a few months ago, bruh chill I'm not in an playing mood right now Bark tells him as he slowly walks into his aunt house on 8th st man I don't wanna hear that shit you let them nigga's ride up and shoot you in the ass and you ain't gonna do shit, Snap says continuing to jail off Bark using the part from menace to society movie when Kane homies asked him how he was gonna let his cousin murders just ride up an smoke his cousin, what? I got them that's on burgundy lane Bark replies swearing on their gang, how you gonna do that and they all dead but the dude Pete and he's locked up I heard Snap tells him, word up? damn you handled the situation already Bark asked a little happy that the situation was taken care of and he didn't have to get his hands dirty Nah after they shot you they got into a police chase and crashed and the dude's ty and shooter died from it Snap tells Bark up-dating him, that's krazy Bark says while slowly taken a seat in the living-room, so what you gonna do about it? Snap asked What do you mean? Ty and shooter dead and Pete is locked up what am I supposed to do? Bark asked Nigga they got homies out here on the street's we could go put some work in on them tonight Snap tells him, but I'm not all the way good yet Bark complained, nigga we gonna be in an car you're hand still work right? Snap asked getting upset because Bark is trying to back outta retaliating on them, ight just get a car Bark says but not meaning the words that just came outta his mouth, that's my boy we already got an car parked so as soon as my little brother come from the store we gonna ride and check shit out Snap tells Bark gassed up that he's about to put his murder game down tonight, I thought you said tonight Bark questions, I said we just gonna ride through chill the fuck out Snap says getting more upset at Bark because he's on some bitch shit in Snap eye's.

UMD, N.J HOSPITAL

So Mr. Johnson you don't know who shot you last night? Det.Killburg question's Tone once again officer like I told you before I was at club all-stars last night and some shots went off and I got shot in the back he tells him, so if you were all the way in Elizabeth why didn't you go to an hospital out their? Det.Jackson asked look man I just got in my car and came straight here once I realize I was shot Tone replied, so you drove all the way here by yourself Det.Killburg asked yeah Tone replied so where is your car at? Det.Killburg asked fuck Tone says to himself Tone realize he just fucked up, I want my lawyer man I ain't got nothing else to says to y'all Tone tells them, ok have it your way then Det.Killburg tells him closing the notebook he was writing in to take Tone statement, look son we just here to help but if you don't want our help that's understandable Det.Jackson tells him, man I'm about to go to sleep Tone tells them closing his eyes let's go jack we're outta here Det.Killburg says and walks out the hospital room, Det. Jackson looks at Tone one more time and shakes his head an makes exit out the room closing the door behind him.

TONE

Once they are out the room and Tone hears the door shut he sits up in the hospital bed and takes out his cell phone, and sends a quick text to Dollar, yo did you find out who them nigga's were last night Tone texts him, yeah bruh the word around town is it was them tp nigga Dollar text back a few second later, ight I'll be getting my discharge papers tomorrow tell the crew strap up we going to war Tone text back and powers off the phone and tucked it back under his pillow it was no need to wait for a reply because once Tone said something that's what it was.

MEANWHILE IN MIAMI

Qwae-ma slow down Bar-man yells to his twin as they ride the jet ski's they rented for the day, Qwae-ma turns around and sticks her tongue out at her brother and takes back off riding the jet ski like she's been riding them all her life, but she really just learned how to ride it an half-hour ago Mommy said you were back to your old self but she ain't say you done turned crazy Bar-man says to himself

V-NASTY & KINTAHE

Look at my baby girl go V-nasty says as she and her husband watch the twins ride the jet ski's out in the open ocean, how about we go rent us two of them thing's and join them out their Kintahe say I thought you're never ask let's go V-nasty tells her husband damn near leaving him on the way.

NA-JAY & DA GIRL'S

What are y'all down here talking about this morning Na-jay asked the three women as he walked into the kitchen where Erica is hard at work making break-fast and Lisa and Lady-red sits at the table talking, oh nothing really I'm just telling them about the old man that's all Lisa replied talking for the other two, you talking to them about him what you should be doing is talking to him or texting him, I need you to get close to him asap I'm trying to have this job done and over with Na-jay tells her taken a seat at table I'm a get on it right now Lisa tells him and reaches for her Iphone that lays on the table, red how's the little homies like that dope we got from Tommy Na-jay asked, they said the shit fire but it doesn't have no stamp on it Lady-red replied, I know I gotta get around to that thing's just been moving fast lately Na-jay tells her I know the shit already Lady-red say damn Erica what you over their cooking up some coke? I'm hunger is hell Na-jay tells her I cooked up all the coke last night but you gotta wait shit not done yet damn Erica tells him while flipping the bacon over in the pan, outta three of the females Erica is the most outspoken one when Na-jay goes into one of his moods and start tripping she'll trip out right back on him, these three females all love Na-jay they all share the same bed with him also they not only share the bed together with him but they also share him and not one of them sees nothing wrong with this situation neither women has low self-confidence about they self all three of them are sexy in their own way, Lisa coming in 5'7 light brown skin Hazel eyes with an amber rose haircut, Erica 5'5 dark skin long black hair down with a body like buffy for Lady-red who's real name is Malikah she looks just like pinky they both would pass for twins, Na-jay met them out west a few years back when he went to visit the homies all three of them were robber's, the homies introduce Na-jay to them and Na-jay fell into an love type of friendship with them because Na-jay never met three women that came off like them and the stories he was told about them just added more to it so Na-jay stayed in-tune with them through out all year's, and once Fat-kat got killed Na-jay had no one else to trust in the city, so he called and offered them a new life which turned out not to be any better than the ones they were already living, but they came anyway, for a few reasons for one they never been to new-jersey and for two they were all on the most wanted list in california for multiple robberies and murders, so they would had jumped at the chance to leave cali, Na-jay offer just came at the right time because their money was getting low and their picture's stayed on the news all the time, so it was either come to new-jersey or stay in cail on the run until somebody ratted out their whereabouts.

JABB

Tae what's good? Jabb asked Tae-tae once she walked through the visit door to see him, nothing much, you know I had to come through and see my baby, Tae-tae replied, oh so now I'm your baby Jabb asked playing around with her, fool you know the shit, you been my baby from day one Tae-tae tells him meaning every word she just said to him, yeah I know the shit but how did the job interview go yesterday? Jabb asked well for one I got the job and for two you should had called yesterday to find out what happened Tae-tae say Nah baby I was type stressing yesterday and just felt like being by myself Jabb replied, Jabb that's so fucking selfish of you were suppose to be one what you go through is what I go through and when I go through something it should be the same way in your eyes Tae-tae say Bay you don't understand Jabb replied, well help me to understand then? Is it the case's you're fighting? Tae-tae says, nah I was stressing over Banger Jabb tells her, what? You're really bugging the fuck out, not for nothing Banger was an snitch and you're stressing over him do you hear how you sound right now? Tae-tae say in Tae-tae book and where she was from which is avon if you snitch on anyone even an crackhead you're supposed to die, he was an snitch tells Jabb, but he was my brother Jabb tells her getting real loud in his visit booth letting everybody hear his conversation, Jabb you sound like a fool right now Banger is the reason you are in here and not only you also you're homie's, but the lady just knocked on the door so I guess our 15 minutes visit is done, but I'll come see you saturday I don't start the job at the bank until monday Tae-tae tells Jabb ight I'll call you tonight Jabb replied, I love you Tae-tae tells him holding open the visit door, love you more Jabb tells her, as Jabb makes his way back down the stairs from his visit he just had his thoughts are on the conversation he just had with Tae-tae, damn she is right he I'm stressing over Banger being dead and he was telling on me to save himself, after Banger was murdered Tae-tae and Jabb became tight she was therefore Jabb when he was home coming to his mother house to check on him because she knew how much Banger getting killed hurt Jabb, and they were both going through it over losing a loved one, with Tae-tae cousin Rain getting killed then Banger getting killed right after, with Tae-tae and Jabb being around each other so much they became one overnight, awww fuck Jabb yells due to somebody throwing hot water in his face, Jabb goes to grab his face which was the dumbest thing he could had done because his face skin comes right off into his hands, Jabb opens his eyes and sees a punch coming right at him, then he feels another one to the back of his head, oh shit nigga's tripping Jabb says to himself, but it's too late for him to do anything but ball up and hope the police get's here fast to stop whoever is jumping him, being as Jabb is the only tp homie on his pod know one comes to help him, as Jabb lays balled up on the floor he's trying to understand why he's being jumped the only people that knows why he's being jumped right now is the ten phantom homie's who's kicking and punching him.

BH

Yeah Speedy shit kind of fucked up for us, but they ain't really got nothing on us but they still tryna stick the Rico law on us all they got is the snitch nigga Banger statements but he's dead, so we're going all the way BH tells the old stick up kid name Speedy who's now nothing but a glass dick smoking crack head, I know the game lil soldier I gave back them 35 years they gave me for all them robberies back in the day, but BH you got an lighter for an old gangster? Speedy asked, yeah what you got tho? BH asked looking forward to smoking some tobacco, I just got these 3 nicks of crack I got in Speedy replied while showing BH the three small bag's of crack, BH eye's light up as he lock eyes with the small bags of crack in Speedy hand, I'm saying you tryna sell that BH asked trying to get the crack from Speedy so he could smoke it by himself, hell no young gangster I'm smoking this shit Speedy replied, ight I got an lighter but you gonna bring me in? BH asked Bring you in? What you mean? You tryna smoke this shit with me? Speedy asked a little to loud, BH looked out his cell window to see if any of the little homie's heard Speedy, satisfied that no one heard him, BH turns back around, yeah I'm a smoke it with you BH tells him, you sure man? Speedy asked, yeah I'm sure BH replied fast due to him ready to smoke the crack, ight put up the block and let's get to it Speedy tells him while laying the crack on the desk table in the cell, so they could break up the crack and smoke it like an blunt.

5-MINUTES LATER BH

Boom, boom, ayo BH the co wants you, Lil Rah-rah tells him from the other side of BH cell door, what? BH asked taken down the window block, the co wants you Lil Rah-rah tells BH again, damn what's that smell? Lil Rah-rah asked, mind your business BH tells him while opening his cell door and walking pass him toward the co desk What's good? Lil soldier Speedy asked coming to the cell door with his eye's all glassy, yo what was y'all smoking Lil Rah-rah asked, lil soldier that's crack you're smelling Speedy tells him thinking he's schooling Lil Rah-rah on something but he's putting BH out their, so y'all was smoking crack Lil Rah-rah asked surprised by this news, yeah we were smoking crack you smell it right? Speedy replied shaking his head and then walking pass Lil Rah-rah, young dumb nigga's Speedy says to hisself and makes his way to the gym for some fresh air, damn big bruh smoking crack Lil Rah-rah says to himself damn I gotta let Ju know this shit Lil Rah-rah says and takes off to find Ju.

BEAR

Malikah why the fuck you going through my phone Bear asks his girlfriend catching her looking through his cell phone, what? I wasn't looking thru your phone Malikah tells him lying, so why the fuck do you have my phone in your hand then? If you wasn't looking through it? Bear says while sitting up in the bed he shares with her, I thought it was ringing Malikah replies lying again, man give me my shit Bear tells her, no body wasn't going through you're shit Malikah replied and throws the phone at Bear which lands on his chest, keep playing with me I'm a bust you're shit open Bear says meaning every word, nigga I wish you would Malikah says while standing up from sitting on the edge of their bed, and where the fuck you think you're going Bear asked oh I'm going to my people's house I'll see you later

Malikah tells him making her out the bed room, and who's you're people's? Bear questions her, and wouldn't you like to know? Malikah replied while leaving Bear to think about where she was going, I'm a beat this bitch ass one day Bear says to himself while going thru his phone to see if he slipped up and left some evident in his phone from any of his jump off.

OLD-MAN

Who the fuck you texting? the old man wife Nikki asked catching him off guard, I'm texting one of my lil homie the old man tells her lying, the old man is really texting Lisa, rich you keep playing games with me, my word I'm a cut your ass up Nikki tells the old man calling him by his real name, nik I'm not playing no games with you this really bone of my lil homie the old man replied trying to calm Nikki down because he knew she'll truly try to cut him, well you need to put whoever that is on hold an get ready so we could go to ihop Nikki tells him Ihop? the Old-man says sitting up in the bed and putting his phone to the side, what you forgot? Nigga last night you promise me we'll go to ihop in the morning and you're not about to talk yourself outta this one so let's go Nikki tells the old man ight I'm getting up now the old man tells her picking back up his phone so he could take it into the bathroom with him while he takes a shower just in case Nikki wanted to check it while he was taken an shower, why you taking your phone with you? What you got something to hide? Nikki asked nah I don't gt nothing to hide I wanna take the phone with me just in case AJ call I wanna be able to answer the old man replied telling the truth about AJ call but lying about the dirt he's hiding in his iphone, what's going on with AJ and his crazy ass brother anyway? Nikki asked before the old man could make it outta the bedroom, they good he should be going up for an bail hearing because the judge never set one for none of them, so they all should be getting one this wednesday the old man replied I hope he does Nikki says I do to the old man tells her and makes his way to the bathroom, Nicki thoughts goes to AJ after the old man leaves the room, Nikki and AJ became cool when the old man caught his last bid, they weren't always cool due to the fact that Nikki thought it was AJ fault that the Old-man ran the street's because they were always together, but once the old man went down AJ always made sure to check on her and gave her money for the Old-man and herself every week, and outta everything AJ never tried to come on to her so in Nikki book AJ was a true brother to her and also an real nigga, Nikki always thought to herself if she never dealt with the old man she would not had mind giving AJ a try, and from what the old man told Nikki about how AJ wife Kim been coming Nikki might just have to put one of her home-girl's on AJ being as though she couldn't have him.

KIM

AJ sit your ass down before I whip your little ass Kim tells her son due to him keep standing up in the visit waiting hall seat's mommy where my daddy at? Lil AJ asked Boy we about to see him in a minute Kim tells him excuse me a female voice says to Kim, may I help you? Kim asked real smart because she's still upset about last night and is not beat for no one right now and all she wants to do is talk to AJ before his homie's does because she knows what they think they also wasn't that and she wants to set things straight, I'm sorry I just wanted to say your son is real handsome the young women sitting next to Kim say thank you lil AJ replies before his mother could thank her, Kim and the young women both bust out laughing at lil AJ, hello my name is Lexi the young women tells Kim while sticking out her hand for an friendly hand shake, and mines Kim, Kim replied shaking Lexi hand, how long do we gotta wait to see our people's Kim asked it was just an code from my understanding but they should be calling people any minute this you're first time coming to see somebody in this jail? Lexi says yeah but I'm here to see my husband Kim says that's what's up? Lexi replied a Lexi come here Lexi cousin Angie yells out loud in the visit waiting hall that's my crazy ass cousin calling me nice meeting Lexi says standing up from her seat well nice meeting you Kim replied nice meeting you to and bye handsome Lexi tells lil AJ bye bye lil AJ tells her standing up in his seat again, boy sit your ass down Kim tells him pulling him into his seat, mommy I gotta use the bathroom lil AJ tells Kim let's go boy Kim tells him grabbing him by his small hand.

CASH & DOLLAR

Bruh they fuck with the wrong nigga's I promise you if I ever see anyone of them pussy boys it's on sight I swear to god Cash yells out loud as him Dollar and some of their all out crew sit in the living room of one of their many honeycombs, dig I talk to Tone earlier and he wants everybody ready for war when he gets out the hospital I also got all the information we need on them nigga's from last night at the club Dollar tells the crew, and may I ask how you came about this information paper boy asked while rolling up a blunt of weed, a few Dollars to the right people and you could find out whatever you wanna know Dollar says cracking a smile at paperboy due to the inside joke about a few dollar's so when we riding out Cash asked ready to get to the situation at hand, as soon as Tone gets out the hospital we riding out Dollar tells him, ight I'm a call my little cousin Shorty and tell him get us some car's cash replied while putting the ice pack he been holding on one of his black eyes, ight do that because we need to have everything ready by the time bruh get out the hospital Dollar tells him before leaving out the living-room, I'm a kill them nigga's cash says while strolling through his phone for his little cousin Shorty number.

AJ & KRAZY J

Bruh how you just gonna throw that nigga up under me? You should of put him under little Rico Krazy J tells his brother, look little bruh the dude Sav knows a lot of info we need about Na-jay and we can't trust little Rico to keep watch on him or to find out what we need to know and lil Rico is only 21yrs old Sav is way older than him, and he might be a couple steps a head of Rico streetwise so I need you on to him AJ tells his lil brother, AJ ayo AJ lil Rico yells to AJ yeah AJ replied from sitting at the table with his brother in the day room of the pod, they called our names for visit lil Rico tells AJ, damn oh girl really came to see you Krazy J say word up shit I can't even get Kim to come see me and her name been on my list from day one of me being in this jail, but I'm a let you know about this chick Lexi when I get back and I'm a see if she got an friend for you AJ tells his brother, ight bruh I'm about to play chess Krazy J replied standing up from the table they been sitting at.

KIM

Yes ms the officer at the visit hall waiting area told me they called my husband name he told me to come down this way and give you this paper Kim tells the co lady while handing her the small visiting paper after the co takes the paper from Kim she looks at it, I just saw this name the co say to herself one of those doors right there the co tells Kim pointing to the visit door, thank you Kim replied grabbing lil AJ by the hand, once Kim get's to the visit door she sees it's already somebody inside the room ms It's already some body inside this visit room Kim tells the co, is it you're husband the co replied sitting back at her desk, no Kim replied and if it was it would had been some shit Kim says to herself, well go to the next door and see if he's in that one the co replied, what the fuck Kim says out loud getting an shock of her life, mommy you said a bad word lil AJ tells Kim.

AJ & LEXI

You funny is hell AJ tells Lexi due to her telling him about a lil boy she saw in the waiting area that looked just like him that may been his son, AJ eye's pops out like he's seeing a ghost right now him and Kim are both stuck looking at each other, AJ can't believe Kim is standing on the other side of the visit door looking at him, and Kim can't believe AJ has some other women here seeing him, what? Lexi asked to an shock looking AJ slowly Lexi turns around and she can't believe her eye's it's the female Kim who she just met in the visit hall waiting area with the lil boy who she just was telling AJ might be his son.

KIM

Open this fucking door Kim yells out loud making a scene for all the people inside the other visiting room's who are now looking out the small visit windows, all you gotta do is turn the knob the co tells Kim while still sitting at her desk waiting for the show that she's sure is about to start, at the essex county jail thing's like this always happen a inmate is always getting caught up with two girl friends showing up at the same time and it'll be on in the hallway with both women fighting over these inmates like cat's and dog's What the fuck is this? Kim asked once she opened the door, daddy lil AJ yells happy to finally see his father, what? Yo you need to chill out with all that yelling AJ tells Kim trying to keep her from causing even more of an scene, so this what you doing now Kim asked AJ while pointing at Lexi who stands their still in shock and can't believe that the women she just somewhat be friend husband is the same person she's here to see, man go head with that bs this my friend AJ tells Kim, you're friend? oh so now we got friend's? Kim asked Wasn't you with a friend last night at the club? AJ question's Kim, look AJ I guess this is a bad time so I'm just gonna leave Lexi say Know you could stay because I'm leaving Kim says grabbing lil AJ by the hand and stepping back outta the visit room, man fuck that bitch AJ tells Lexi, Kim hears him right before the door shuts mommy I wanna go back and see my daddy lil AJ tells Kim, know baby we're leaving Kim tells him breaking down crying while they walk thru the hallway, I knew he was gonna believe their story but I ain't think he'll move on this fast Kim says to herself.

DET. KILLBURG & DET. JACKSON

So Killburg how did you come to meet Vickie? Det.Jackson asked It's a long story Det.Killburg replied not really wanting to tell Det. Jackson how he met Vickie, don't tell me you pulled that old trick of pulling her over and getting her number Det.Jackson asked laughing at his own joke, Det.Killburg doesn't try to correct him because Det. Jackson is somewhat right about how he met Vickie a few months back Det.Killburg was patrolling one late night by himself due to him doing over time he notice a red v6 accord swerving from side to side Det.Killburg than activated his light's to pull the car over, which pulled off to the side of the road on Springfield Ave and 12th st in Newark N.J After calling in to dispatch and running the vehicle plates the driver came back as a female Vickie towns from Newark N.J Det.Killburg still approached the vehicle with cautious the driver rolled down the window relieving a light skin female who eyes were bloodshot red miss are ok Det.Killburg asked her concerned for the women because it was either she been crying or was very intoxicated I'm ok why do you asked that officer Vickie asked voice sluggish which let's him know the woman is truly under the influence of something, miss have you been drinking? Det.Killburg, Vickie breaks down crying because she knows she's going to jail tonight for dwi, miss why are you crying Det.Killburg asked Vickie again, yes I have been drinking and maybe a little to much Vickie tells the police officer, Vickie is not only crying because she's been drinking she's also is crying because she has her 380 under her leg and she knows if the police officer tells her to step out the car he's gonna see the small pistol on the seat miss can you please but before Det.Killburg could ask Vickie for her paper work Vickie cuts him officer I'll do anything please don't take me to jail Vickie tells him What did you say? Det. Killburg asked face turning red due to Vickie disrespecting him like he was some type of trick, I said I'll do anything please don't take me to jail Vickie says again, Det.Killburg thinks it over for an second, alright this how you wanna play Det.Killburg says to himself, what do you have to offer Det.Killburg playing along with Vickie, I'll suck off Vickie replied Det.Killburg takes a step back because he's shock by Vickie statement, how about some pussy along with that Det.Killburg asks, Vickie drops her head and Det.Killburg thinks he pushed to far and losted Vickie along the way, ok meet me at the days inn on 1&9 I'm in room 227 I'll be there waiting for you Vickie tells him and takes off in her v6 accord leaving Det.Killburg standing on the side of the road watching her car tail lights At first Det.Killburg tells himself he's not gonna show up than his little head starts to think for him letting his big head know that he never been with a black women before and to go see if the saying was true if you go black you never go back From that on Vickie been Det.Killburg somewhat girlfriend Hey kill-brug are you ok? Det.Jackson asked him catching him zoned out, what? oh yeah yeah I'm good my mind was just some where else that's all Det. Killburg replies, yeah I see that Det.Jackson replied while driving the unmarked police car.

NA-JAY, ERICA, LISA & LADY-RED

Lady-red make this right turn on sunset Iwanna see if my lil mans out here Na-jay tells her, how are we about to put in some work and you wanna do pop up's on people Erica say what I tell you about you and you're mouth Na-jay replies from the passenger seat of the rented truck they are in, na she is right Lisa says jumping into the conversation, here you go, don't you got somebody you need to be texting or talking to Na-jay say I been texting him all day he's out with his wife at ihop eating Lisa replied Which one they at Lady-red asked while driving the rented black tinted loose tahoe truck, he ain't say Lisa replied, well make up an story or something tell him one of your cousin work at ihop but say which one but let him know you're cousin would make his bill cheaper Lady-red tells her, alright but y'all ain't gotta be teaming up on me Lisa replied all in her feelings but texting the old man at the same time with the story about her cousin working at ihop, damn he ain't out here Na-jay says looking in the face's of all the dude's standing on the corner in front of the poppy store, Na-jay you really got us on some body block looking for some corner boy? Erica says with an look of dislike on her face due to her looking at the corner boy's Here you're smart ass go again I guess you need some act right Na-jay replied talking about having sex, one of the rules Na-jay and the three women made up was they were not to have sex with anyone body outside of each other, the catch to it was they didn't want to catch feelings for any outsider's this rule was ok with Na-jay due to the fact that he could have sex with any of them some times with all of them at the same time, he texted me back Lisa let them all know, so which one he at? Na-jay asked ready to finally put his choppa to work today, he said he at the one in Irvington Lisa replied not saying irvington right and also having know clue where the old man was at due to her not being from this state, it's irvington Na-jay tells correcting her I'm not from here so I could care less about how you say it Lisa tells him, it's not my fault you country Na-jay tells her trying to be funny, whatever fool Lisa replied, are we gonna kill this fool or are we just gonna ride around in this truck full of gun's for know reason Erica say Lady-red once you get to sandford make a left turn we gonna ride it all the way out to Springfield Ave I hate riding up 18th ave Erica says and whys that? Na-jay asked because state police always riding this block Erica replied and where the fuck you see the state boy's at Na-jay asked right behind us Erica tells him once those words left her mouth everybody in the truck turned in their seat to see for their self and they get the shock of their life it's not just one state police car behind them it's an tRain of them behind them, yo chill out Lady-red says as she drives the truck real careful now pulling to the red light, word up everybody be cool Na-jay tells the crew while turning back around in his seat heart racing Na-jay knows if the state police try to pull them over it's gonna be a long chase the state police has the fastest cop car's and not only that they also shoot first and ask questions last but the real problem is Na-jay isn't driving and he's the only one that knows these street's inside the truck and him telling Lady-red which way to turn in a police chase can be real difficult, we good they turning off Lady-red tells them watching her mirror's, you wanna drive Lady-red ask Na-jay who's checking his side mirror's nah I trust you're wheel baby girl, but hurry up doe so we won't miss this nigga leaving ihop Na-jay tells her You're scary ass Erica says out loud hoping to start back up with Na-jay but he doesn't pay her any mind.

V-NASTY & KIM

Ms.V I'm so done with your son he really had another girl there to see him, I told myself the other day I wasn't gonna take our son to that place and I still did now look what he had to witness his father getting an visit from another woman Kim tells V-nasty as she sit inside her car in front of her parents house, look Kim that's my son and all but when ever he calls me and him gonna have a long talk about this because I'm not feeling this at all V-nasty replies, but Kim why don't you call him yourself and talk to him? V-nasty asks V-nasty how am gonna call him he's locked up? Kim replied, I know he's locked up but him and that brother of his have a cell phone don't ask he how they got it V-nasty say Kim is surprised by this information oh so that might be all these voicemail I have it might be him that left they Kim says, well check them and see if it's him if not I'll text you the number V-nasty tells Kim but msv if he calls you make sure you let him know the guy last night at the club I ain't know him Kim tells V-nasty trying to plead her case to V-nasty again, baby don't worry yourself V-nasty replied, ok ma love you Kim says love you to V-nasty replies before ending their call

Kim hopes V-nasty is able to talk to AJ because she doesn't wanna lose her husband to that young girl that was at the visit, but right now Kim needs to be around family that's why she's in front of her parent's house later on she'll call Toya for some friendly support.

SNAP, BARK & SHORTY

Shorty you need to stop playing games and come under this burgundy land wave it's about overdue for you everybody in our city banging but you Snap tells him, bruh I fucks with you why I gotta bang for it's 2016 it's kind of late for me to join any gang now been getting by this long without banging why should I do it now Shorty asked Snap while he drove the stolen four door e550 benz through Osborne Terr Snap he ain't gotta bang this gang shit not for everybody anyway Bark says coming to Shorty aid, bruh nobody not talking to you Snap tells Bark mad that he's coming in between him trying to bring Shorty under Shorty burgundy lane, Snap me driving for y'all should let you know I'm down with y'all already and I'm not charging y'all for nothing Shorty tells Snap trying to get him to understand he'll ride for him without him being under their gang, hold on my phone ringing Shorty tells them reaching for his phone inside the cup-holder, yo what's good? Shorty says into the phone, yo little cousin where you at? Cash asked over the other end of the phone I'm with my man's right now Shorty tells him while making a right turn off Osborne Terr on to Hawthorne Ave heading toward Na-jay building's ayo I need you to come through for me I need some car's asap cash tells him, I only got one car right now and we about to use it Shorty replies ayo who that? Snap asked due to Shorty telling who ever he talking to their business, this my cousin Shorty replied, man who the fuck is that asking questions? Cash asked getting mad because somebody was getting into him and Shorty business, that's my man's Snap Shorty replied, I don't know that nigga, but anyway I need some wheel's lil cousin cash tells Shorty again, and I need some money Shorty tells him, damn cuz you gonna charge me for some stolen car's I thought we were family cash replies we are family but you know this how I eat, and I bet if I wanted some work you'll charge me right? Shorty says, Cash gets quiet because he knows what Shorty just said is true aight how much you gonna charge me? cash asked damn how many you need? Shorty asked I need 5 of them cash replied ight give me a rack for each car Shorty replied, aight aight I got you hit me when you get them and make sure they all machine's cash tells him, nigga you know all I drive is machine's Shorty replied while taking the blunt of rolled up weed from Snap hold before we end this I might need you to drive for me to Cash tells Shorty, aight I got you I'll do this one for free but next time you paying me Shorty tells him, ight be safe cash says aight you to cuz Shorty replied ending the call, ayo you bringing me in on selling them car's? Snap asked Shorty I got you bruh long as you help me steal them Shorty say hell yeah I'll help you get them Snap replies, damn Snap you always want in on something Bark says from the back seat, hell yeah if it's money to be made I want in Snap replied, yo their go some of them nigga's right their Bark tells them, I see them Snap replied while looking at all the face's of the phantom dude's standing in front of the building on the 500 block of Hawthorne Ave so what y'all wanna do? Shorty asked as he makes an left turn so he could double back around the block in case Snap and Bark wanted to handle their business now, nah my lil brother wanna play to so we gonna wait until tonight and we not about to do know drive by we popping out on these nigga's Snap tells Shorty like the situation at hand is over him and not Bark getting shot, aight son what we gonna do in the meantime? Shorty asked Let's go see if we could get them car's because a nigga is in need of some money Snap says taking the blunt brak just passed him, aight I'm about to jump on rt78 we gonna shoot to Milburn and see if we could catch something Shorty tells them, cool by me Snap says while leaving his seat back.

OLD-MAN & NIKKI

Thank you and have a nice day the waitress at ihop tells the Old-man and his wife, let's go because I need to get the fuck away from you because if you text you're so call little homie who you claim to been texting one more time I'm a kill you're ass Nikki tells the Old-man, bae I just showed you who I was texting the Old-man tells her, nigga I don't know who you think you're fooling you could of saved who-ever the bitch you been texting name under any-name Nikki replies, Nikki doesn't know how right she is right now because that's what the Old-man did saved Lisa number under the name bang boy, aight let's go because I'm tired of you're shit I told you it was my little man's texting me about a situation going on the Old-man tells her as they walked outta ihop towards his wife 2016 bmw x6 jeep neither of them paying any attention to nothing going on around them, oh so now you mad? miss me with that shit Nikki says unlocking the truck.

NA-JAY, ERICA, LISA & LADY-RED

There he go right their Lisa says pointing the old man out to them, what we gonna get him right now? Erica asked Na this parking lot to small if we start letting these choppas go everybody gonna be running all over the place and it's gonna be hard to pull outta this parking lot on Springfield Ave with all the traffic, but some as he pulls to any red light we gonna chop they ass down, Na-jay tells them, so we killing her to Lisa asked feeling a little sorry for the women who the Old-man has with him because nine times outta ten the women has know dealing with nothing the Old-man has going on, bullet's don't got know names on them if she get hit she gets hit Na-jay replied.

OLD-MAN & NIKKI

Yo let me get your truck tinted for you, I'm tired of riding with you in this fish bowl the old man tells his wife, nah I'm good nobody is looking for me or I don't have know reason to hide behind tinted windows, Nikki replied as she pulled to the light on Springfield Ave and Sandford.

NA-JAY & THE GIRL'S

Damn Na I gotta pull up on the driver side due to her being in the right lane Lady-red tells him, aight hurry up we just about to chop up the driver side I know we gonna hit him also these choppa's going through the doors of that jeep and once we're done bust the left turn at the light it's know way we're gonna be able to go down Springfield Ave pass the Irvington police station Na-jay tells Lady-red, aight get ready lady's it show time Erica says cocking her baby choppa back.

OLD-MAN & NIKKI

Yeah just drop me off on my block and you can come back and get me later I'm not in the mood to be driving today the Old-man tells Nikki, yeah whatever you might be having you're next bitch pick you up from you're block Nikki replies the Old-man turns to Nikki to check her about her mouth but what he turns to and see is two black machine guns sticking out the window of a black suv truck and one masked person out the sunroof of the truck, pull off, pull off the old man yells at Nikki What? Nikki asked but her words are cut short before she can ask anything else due to the gun fire from the machine guns boom, boom, boom bloc, bloc, bloc boom, boom, boom the first couple shots tear through Nikki body bloc, bloc, bloc the Old-man get hit multiple times but he still tries his best to stay awake and pull Nikki's body under his, what the Old-man doesn't know is it's over for Nikki she'd dead already boom, boom, boom the last thing the Old-man hears are the tire's burning rubber from the truck before his light's go out due to all the bullet's he took.

KRAZY J & AJ

J boss main medical the co yells out to Krazy J, what the fuck I ain't put in no sick call slip for medical Krazy J tells his brother as they sit at the table and talk about what just took place earlier at visit, you didn't? well refuse that shit then AJ tells him, nah I'm going somebody might be tryna holla at me about something Krazy J replied or some body could be tryna pop you AJ adds letting his brother know it could be either one of those, man I'm going I'll see you when I get back Krazy J says letting AJ know its his choice and letting his cockieness take over aight be safe AJ let's him know and zoning back out over the situation with his wife fuck her AJ tells his-self again.

MAIN MEDICAL AREA 5 MINUTES LATER

Yo Krazy what's good? Big bruh Ju asked nothing much Krazy J replied, Krazy J whats good? bruh lil rah rah say you know the shit lil bruh Krazy J tells him, yo I am going to have to get up with y'all in a minute I'm about to find out the reason the doctor called me down here Krazy J tells them, hold bruh we the ones that got you called down here we gotta holla at you about two thing's Ju tells Krazy J, ight what's good? Krazy J asked tryna get to the reason why they got him called down to main medical, step over here in this room Ju tells him so the doctor's won't hear what they were about to talk about, what's the problem Krazy J asked once they were inside the little waiting room for the inmates, it's a few thing's Ju tells him well get to it Krazy J tells him getting impatience, aight so you know me and Rah-rah work down here so we get to see mostly everybody and if you go to lock up for a fight they gotta bring you here to make sure you alright but anyway them phantom nigga's jumped Jabb on his pod, and Kk and them got into a big fight on their pod with the phantom nigga's, I got a chance to holla at Kk and them they said it's a stamp on all tp nigga's from them phantom nigga's word is they suppose to eat any and all tp nigga's Ju tells Krazy J some news he already heard some what from Sav, and what else? Krazy J asked Ju and Rah-rah looks at each other and put their heads down neither one of them wants to relay this news to Krazy J because they know BH is also his day one friend and they don't know how he's gonna react to the news, what the fuck is y'all so quiet for now? Krazy J asks while looking at both of them who doesn't want to make eye contact with him big bruh we caught BH smoking crack Lil Rah-rah tells Krazy J, who shakes his head at this information because this is not the first time he heard this information, Bear told AJ and Krazy J this also, aight look I want y'all to pass word to all the bruh's under the hood to move out on all phantom nigga's if they want war that's what we gonna bring and for BH have the homies on y'all pod pop him he's done Krazy J tells them both, Ju and Lil Rah-rah are shock by this but they keep whatever they are thinking to their self because if Krazy J would get a dude he grew up with popped he'll damn sure hit the button on them also, I want y'all to stay out the war if y'all could because I need y'all to keep this job in-case we need to have people called down here Krazy J tells them, aight big bruh we gonna handle it asap lil Rah-rah tells him happy to being trusted for a job for the big homie Krazy J, us Krazy J tells them and makes his way back out of the small room back to his pod so he could let AJ know what's into play now.

LIL RAH-RAH & JU

Damn big bruh really has a cold heart lil Rah-rah tells Ju once Krazy J is gone, word up bruh but they are about to send us back to our pod for count we'll let the homies know what bruh said than Ju says, aight I'm with that lil Rah-rah replied.

BH & SPEEDY

Yo how much do you got left of that shit BH asked Speedy as they walked lap's inside the gym high outta their mind due to smoking another bag of crack Speedy had, damn nigga I only got two nick's of crack left we gotta save some for later Speedy says a little to loud for BH liking damn bruh why you always gotta be so loud? BH asked man fuck these nigga's so what we smoke crack Speedy says letting everybody in on their business, yo chill the fuck out BH tells him while looking around the gym to see who's paying him and Speedy any attention, yo how bad Tina doing out their? BH asked changing the subject, who? Bad-Tina? oh she's doing good she's in rehab now they said you're people's the Old-man sent her Speedy says why would he do that? BH asked feeling some type of way about the Old-man sending bad-Tina away to get her shit together, BH now thinks the Old-man wants bad-Tina for himself, why else would a person send somebody to rehab but to help them Speedy tells him, but you should be happy for her Speedy adds I am BH replies lying.

BIG-DAWG & TOMMY

Ayo Tommy, Tommy Big-dawg yells as he runs outta the office of the car lot they have on 1&9 hwy What? Tommy asked as he pulls the 2015 Audi s8 to a stop, what? I'm about to pull this shit to the detail side to have it cleaned Tommy tells Big-dawg once he rolled the driver window all the way down, yo Na-jay just hit me and said the job done Big-dawg tells Tommy who's a little surprise by this news, Tommy didn't think Na-jay would have got the job done this fast, did you hear me Na-jay handled that old nigga Big-dawg says again, yeah I heard you let me pull this car around so they can detail it Tommy says while slowly pulling off in the s8, damn it's about to be some shit in the street's of essex county over the old man getting killed Tommy says to himself.

SHORTY, SNAP & BARK

Ayo you want me to park it right here Bark asked Shorty, once he was on the side of him in the 2014 c-class benz, yeah put it right their Shorty replied yo why you parking that shit all the way out here in South Orange Snap question Shorty unsure why they were parking the stolen car out of town, because Newark and Irvington stay on some beat shit running plates on car's all the time, out here it look like it belongs out here right Shorty replied, word up! That shit don't even look stolen Snap tells Shorty while looking around to make sure the police don't creep up on them or know one is watching them from any of the house windows yo so we still gonna play on them fool's tonight Shorty asked Snap as Bark got into the back seat of the stolen cat they were in, nah we gonna keep getting these car's for your cousin money first murder second Snap tells Shorty, that's what I'm talking about Shorty replies and takes off speeding in the stolen car.

TWO WEEKS LATER AJ, BEAR, KRAZY J, GOOBA, & BABY

Yeah bruh we just left the hospital Bear tells AJ was bruh up AJ asked nah he ain't wake up yet Bear replied, so who you with? AJ asked it's me Baby and Gooba Bear tells him, tell them I sent my love AJ say love that nigga back both Gooba and Baby says, yo y'all still haven't found out about who did this shit yet? AJ question's nah bruh the street's been quiet about this shit nobody knows nothing and everybody thinks the Old-man is dead, Bear tells AJ damn they counted my boy out like that? AJ asked, yeah but we tryna keep it that way also Bear says, yeah I know the shit but dig I'm about to hit Tommy up and see if he could help us find out anything AJ replied, bruh don't tell him the Old-man in a coma I don't trust him either because it's funny that after the Old-man told him we weren't gonna be doing business with him know more bruh gets hit up and his wife get killed Bear says, bruh Tommy wouldn't do no shit like this AJ replied taken up for Tommy, ight if you say so but when is the next time you gonna be calling because we having a meeting tonight over the situation we not about to keep sitting around not doing nothing we gotta make somebody pay for what happened to big bruh Bear tells AJ, bruh they got the jail on lockdown due to the code's that kept going off we at war with them phantom nigga's in here I be having the worker charge the phone up once a day but if anything I'll call tomorrow to see what y'all came up with I trust that y'all three would make the right choice AJ tells them, ayo what's going on with y'all bail's Gooba asked we waiting for some check stub's we got the money already AJ replied so y'all should be out of their this week? Gooba asked something like that AJ replies yo that's true about BH? Baby questions Yeah lil bruh pushed the button on him AJ says while shaking his head, AJ didn't agree on the call Krazy J made but it's too late to cry over it now, BH is on pc now AJ tells them, word? that's krazy Bear says, but I'll hit y'all later AJ tells them, yo where you're brother at? Bear ask he sleep AJ tells him while looking at Krazy J who plays sleep, aight tell bruh I love him when he gets up Bear say I'll do that AJ says ending the call, Krazy J and AJ haven't really been talking lately due to the call Krazy J made on BH.

JJ

So you're really gonna play me like this? I was there for you all them year's you were in prison and you just gonna say fuck me just like that? JJ girlfriend Sheila says to him, look you knew I was about to come home so all your dealings with any dude's while I was away should have been cut off before I came home but you still have nigga's calling you're phone all times of the night and day JJ replies, JJ I'm sorry please give me another chance I promise to be good Sheila says, nah I'm good JJ replied while texting Zoe the address where he was at so she could come get him in the rental car he's been paying for who are you texting Jason? Sheila asked calling JJ by his real name, you're questioning me days are over but if you truly wanna know I'm texting my new wife JJ tells her trying to hurt her feelings really JJ it's like that now? Sheila asked aight just get your shit and get out my house Sheila tells him, what it look like I been doing for the last 20 minute's JJ replied oh look my ride down stairs now JJ tells her while showing her the text he just got from Zoe, so you gave that bitch my address? Shelia asked getting even more madder than she already was look I'm out JJ tells her while making his way out the door and outta Sheila life for good which he thinks but he got another thing coming if he thinks Sheila gonna take this disrespect laying down.

ZOE & JJ

So how did she take it? Zoe question once they pulled off from in front of Sheila house on Grove st and Park ave you know how them spanish chick's be tripping but fuck her take me to the house so I could put up my stuff JJ tells her, ok Zoe replied once JJ got outta prison he kept his word and went and got Zoe outta jail, with all the money JJ was making in prison selling dope he was able to pay Zoe bail and rent to own the house they were now about to share together Jason promise you'll never leave me Zoe says to JJ baby girl long as you never lie to me and stay loyal to me I'll never leave you now get out you're bag of feelings I need to get to the hospital before the day is over JJ tells her once JJ got release from prison he went through homebase looking for the Old-man he ran into Bear who told him what happened to the Old-man the news hurt JJ because he wasn't there to protect his big bruh JJ doesn't know Bear and them like that so he stays away from them once AJ comes home he'll come around more JJ knows the game has changed you can't even trust people not even under your own hood because they the one to kill you first and nobody knowing who got at the Old-man just sounds funny the hit had to come from some body close so in JJ book everybody was a suspect until the Old-man opened his eyes and said otherwise.

TONE, DOLLAR & CASH

So we just gonna let that shit ride because somebody killed their big bruh before we did Cash asked upset that Tone was changing the plans look I got shot over the situation I feel some type of way to but us going out killing people that don't really count ain't gonna matter because somebody else just gonna come along and take their place it's pointless is all I'm saying Tone tells Cash, so I gave away 5 stacks for no reason for some fucking stolen cars that we not even gonna use? that's crazy bruh Cash replied first off you need to take it down some second if you still wanna ride out over the shit that happened at all star's go ahead nobody stopping you Dollar say so y'all just gonna let me ride out by myself? Cash asked bruh when you think about it this shit over a bitch that's not neither one of ours but if you wanna ride out fuck it find a driver and we gonna make a movie tonight Tone says getting upset that Cash won't let the situation go that's what I'm talking about Cash says I hope he got the wheel because I'm not trying to go to jail tonight Dollar tells Cash Man my little cousin Shorty got that wheel Cash replies taken up for his cousin I hope so Tone replies.

DET. JACKSON & DET. KILLBURG

So y'all basically do whatever y'all wanna do take breaks any time y'all want? Hazel asked Det.Jackson as she sits across from him at the applebees on Springfield Ave in Newark N.J Yeah something like that Det.Jackson replied are y'all investigating the Old-man and his wife murder Vickie asked tryna find out some information on the Old-man murder so she could have something to run her mouth about when she goes to get her hair done, yeah we're investigating his wife murder why you got some information on what happened to her? Det.Killburg questioned Vickie What? oh no I don't know nothing about what happened to them I told you all I heard about it already Vickie replied all Vickie told Det.Killburg was what the street's were saying which was nothing so y'all only investigating his wife murder and not his Hazel asked trying to also find out information, he's not dead Det.Jackson tells her while taking a bite of his cheese steak he's not dead Vickie and Hazel both says at the same time surprised by this news of the old man being alive yeah he's just in a coma Det. Jackson adds while Det.Killburg watches the women reaction to the news and he's surprised that they didn't know the old man was still alive, oh y'all ain't know that? Det.Jackson asked putting his sandwich down know we didn't know that everybody in the city thinks he's dead Hazel tells him well now you know that ain't true Det.Jackson tells her right before he picked back up his sandwich to take another bite for Vickie she can't wait until tomorrow to come so she could go to Jo hair salon to let all the women in their know this information the benefits of having cop's as your boyfriends Vickie tells herself.

KIM, V-NASTY, QWAE-MA, MS. PAT & TOYA

Ms.V thank you so much for being here you to Qwae-ma Kim tells them both It's ok baby you don't gotta thank us we're family this is what family is for to be their for each other V-nasty tells Kim yeah big sis get outta your feelings Qwae-ma say everybody has been surprise about Qwae-ma new found attitude Qwae-ma turned out to be an outspoken person over night, she says and do whatever she feels leave her alone Qwae-ma talking this bag of feelings stuff Toya tells her while sitting behind her new desk inside the office of Kim's day care that they officially opened up today, baby I'm so happy for you Ms.Pat tells Kim as she walks outta the classroom Kim told her was hers I'm happy to ma Kim replies while putting her head down, oh baby what's wrong Ms.Pat asks Kim while wrapping her arms around Kim holding her tight I just wish AJ was here to enjoy this happiness with us Kim says breaking down crying stop crying all the women tells Kim while forming a group hug around Kim he's gonna be home this week V-nasty tells Kim trying to up lift Kim spirit which doesn't work because AJ and Kim still haven't fixed their situation Kim doesn't wanna see AJ in jail but she diffidently doesn't wanna see AJ with the next female, alright y'all let me go y'all my phone ringing Kim tells them, Hello? Kim says answering her cell phone, yeah we at the daycare now Kim responses yeah your mother and you're sister is here also you wanna talk to them? Kim asks AJ and from that statement that lets everybody know that it was AJ the phone Ms.V and Qwae-ma, AJ said he loves y'all and he said J sent his love too Kim tells relaying AJ message, he's with Kintahe and your lil brother they at the race track, well ok love you Kim tells him before he ends the call on her without telling her he loved her, did he say if they were getting off lock down yet? V-nasty asked no all he said was their bail source hearing is in two days and to tell you to pick them up that tonight Kim tells V-nasty sounding real disappointed why he don't want you to pick them up Qwae-ma asked Kim, It's a long story Kim replies and walks off toward the office well would somebody please let me know what's going on? Qwae-ma says to the remaining women who's watching Kim walk down the hallway.

SNAP, BARK & SHORTY

Yo y'all nigga's funny is hell why y'all always beefing? Shorty asked Snap and Bark as they ride down Elizabeth ave in the stolen super 2014 charge range rover sport that they just got from Newark airport man this nigga always tryna control me and I'm not off that shit Bark replied high outta his mind due to the grams of mollie he just took an hour ago, bruh I'm not tryna hear that shit just roll up Snap tells him again, man I'm not rolling up no more I done damn near rolled up half the oz of sour we been smoking Bark complained yo look I'm a drop y'all off on 8st I gotta go handle something with my cousin Shorty tells them, come on bruh we rolling all day and you gonna kick us out now Snap replies not feeling what Shorty just said about dropping them off I'm a come back through tonight and get y'all Shorty lies once they sold the 5 cars to his cousin Cash for the 5 racks Shorty broke Snap and Bark off even, and once Snap saw that he could make money off of just being around Shorty, Snap tries his best to keep Shorty with him every day Snap even offered Shorty a spared room in his mother house so he'll be able to keep Shorty close Snap even is thinks about changing his hustle to the car game from robbing people but Shorty is no fool he knows Snap is trying to use him that's why after tonight he's gonna try his best to stay outta Snap sight ayo y'all saw the news the other day Bark asked ready to talk about the murder they committed the other day on Hawthorne Ave bruh didn't I tell you to stop talking about that shit Snap yells at him from the front seat of the stolen car, see their you go trying to control me again Bark replied while leaning back in the back seat outta Snap reach in case Snap tried to pop off on him.

ESSEX COUNTY JAIL LOCK UP

Yo y'all nigga's lucky I can't get to y'all I swear on my set I'm a break the first phantom nigga shit I see Pop-off yells out through the side of his cell door, man fuck you're set one of the phantom little homie's yells back, yo Pop stop talking so much we gonna catch these nigga's they can only have us in lock up but for 30 days top Jabb tells him mind your fucking business pussy boy another phantom little homie says trying to disrespect Jabb too ya dead mans pussy and that nigga you call ya big homie Na-jay pussy Lucky yells out his cell door all this back and forth yelling and disrespecting each other has been going on every day each set been disrespecting each other so much they are starting to repeat their selves, I hope all you tp nigga's die along with y'all mother's a phantom dude yells out.

BH

Man this out shit in the fucking way I'm not locking back in send me to lock up BH tells the co who's working on the pc pod he's now on, I don't know where you getting all this gangster shit from but last time I checked this was pc so with that you're hour is up go lock your punk ass in before I put you in your cell myself the co tells BH as he sits behind his desk on the unit phone BH is in shock due to how he just been disrespected by the co, not only has BH lost his brother's AJ, Krazy J and the rest of the homie's but he also lost his respect from people, BH puts his head down and walks to his cell, that's what the fuck I thought the co says to BH as BH walks away, damn I'm done up in this town, you know what fuck it I'm food already so I mind is well do some real food shit and get outta jail, I'm calling the district attorney office tomorrow fuck AJ and his brother and tp BH says to himself rip Banger, BH yells out loud slamming his cell door closed.

PROSECUTOR OFFICE NEWARK N.J

Mr.Pete Wilson please have a seat the black prosecutor female tells Pete once he walked into the small room Mr.Wilson we called in a few favors to have you release to us and I'll tell you now it wasn't easy the head prosecutor of the prosecutor office James Gray tells Pete, but as you see we made it happen Pete just nods his head up and down to what he hears, so this is the deal we're putting you on our payroll from now on you work for the prosecutor office, and we have some paperwork for you to sign that states you are agreeing to work with us and this paper right here just states that you agree to all the things we're asking of you to do, do you understand all this? Prosecutor Gray asks yeah I understand Pete replied not to happy with the agreement that's taken place right now, the 364 they were suppose to give Pete never came through, the state changed it up on Pete telling him either he worked for them or he had to fight the charges he was facing, Pete thought it over and he figured what did he have to lose, his name would be in Na-jay paperwork because of the things he told on him, so if they ever caught Na-jay Pete life was over either way, so the main thing we're asking you to do Pete is bring down 5 people a month, I myself don't care how you do it long as you get it done, and you are to report us here at the prosecutor office and also to Det. Killburg and Det.Jackson they are the Det. for the county of essex this card has both of their house and cell phone numbers use these numbers because it'll be the smart thing to do Mr.Gray tells Pete, while looking into his eyes and if you ever need some money or an apartment let them know or me or her, these are our cards Gray tells Pete while handing him two more cards, and last thing Pete if you are thinking about skipping town lose that idea because I promise you we'll hunt you down and when we do catch you things won't be to nice for you, now sign these papers Mr.Gray tells Pete handing him an pen and a big stack of paperwork which basically states Pete is signing his life over to the government.

NA-JAY, LISA, LADY-RED, & ERICA

So you can't find out what they want you for Lisa asked Na-jay while they sat and looked at his picture on the Newark police most wanted top list, nah I gotta send a lawyer in their to find out for me Na-jay replied while looking at some of the charges that's under his picture, Na didn't Tommy tell you that if you ever got into some trouble with the law to let him know because he got somebody on the inside Lady-red reminds Na-jay, yo you right I'm about to call that nigga right now it's about time we reup on some dope anyway Na-jay replies while dialing Tommy phone number.

TOMMY, BIG-DAWG & AJ

Nah bruh we ain't heard nothing about the old man getting touched Tommy lies to AJ ayo AJ you got my word if we hear anything about it we'll let you know Big-dawg tells him fulling AJ up with false hope, did your father say he heard anything about it? AJ question nah I haven't talked to him in a minute he knows I still feel some type of way about him playing apart in getting you off the streets Tommy replies It's cool bruh that's his job it's no love lost on my end AJ tells him how is your bail looking? Big-dawg asks AJ so they'll be up to date on AJ release, my bail shit paid already you heard? AJ replied both Tommy and Big-dawg are taken back by this news, Big-dawg recovers first that's what it is we will be waiting for you when you get out here Big-dawg say, that's cool but I'm a hit y'all once I touch AJ lets them know, ight much love Big-dawg tells AJ you know the shit AJ replied ending the call.

AJ & KRAZY J

Yo they not right bruh Krazy J says once AJ ends the call he was just on, why you say that? AJ asked thinking his brother is tripping again, bruh once you told them you're bail was paid they stop talking for a minute, then the nigga Big-dawg took over the conversation, what happened to Tommy? what he fell asleep around the same time you said you're bail was paid Krazy J says while shaking his head, word up lil bruh AJ replied agreeing with his brother, lil bruh once we get home we'll try to do our homework on the situation and if we find out that they hiding something about what happened to the old man we gonna tie their ass up and off them but we gonna rob them for all they got AJ tells Krazy J, that's what the fuck I'm talking about now I see you're truly back to the old AJ, Krazy J say for these last few days AJ been telling Krazy J that he's going back to his old ways and from what AJ just told Krazy J knows he means business, Krazy J also thinks from the Old-man getting shot and almost killed that has AJ heart going back cold, but that's not the only reason AJ heart is going cold but the situation with Kim has his heart going cold also, AJ doesn't give a fuck about nothing or no one anymore besides his moms and brother's and sister, yo what's good with little Lexi? Krazy J,J asked I'm about to call baby girl she supposed to went to new york for the weekend on some family trip AJ replied, so you really gonna fuck with her when you get out their? Krazy J asks yeah what do I got to lose AJ replies while calling Lexi phone Yeah aight we'll see Krazy J say.

LATER ON THAT NIGHT

This they area you could catch them through any of these blocks from Springfield Ave to 14th ave Shorty tells all his passengers inside the stolen heml cherokee that he sold to his cousin weeks back, damn you must really know these nigga's? Tone questions Shorty not feeling right about putting in work with a dude who knows the other side so well yeah I know some of them I sold them some cars also Shorty says as they ride down 18th st towards 18th ave damn they deep is hell out here Dollar says from the front passenger seat as they he notices the people standing around talking on the block yo that's them nigga's right their cash says as he spots Black and Bear standing on the sidewalk with the group of people, which ones? Shorty ask trying to find out who cash was talking about, the black ass short one with the shortcut and the long beard with the white true religion t-shirt on Cash replies and who else? Shorty asks the big black dude with the dreads cash says pointing out the second person he got into it with at the club, cash would never forget their face's Shorty is happy that cash picked out Bear, no Shorty doesn't have to get his hands dirty by killing Bear not that he really wanted to anyway, aight the first person you picked out his name is Black and the second dude is Bear Shorty tells Cash as they sit at the red light on 18th st and 18th ave waiting for the light to change well it's about to be rip in front of both of their names Cash say while cocking back his mac 11 with the 60 round clip yo it's to many people out their I know these nigga's strap out here Tone says looking out the back window of the jeep that's cool we strap to Cash says not caring if they got into a shootout with Bear and his homie's long as he got to get some get back on them for jumping him at the club, Tone we good Dollar tells him, Tone Snaps outta his super cautions mood asap aight fuck it bust this right and pull over we gonna walk back around this corner and air all their ass's out Tone say that's the Tone I know Cash says ready to murder whoever is out on the block tonight.

BEAR, BLACK, BABY, & GOOBA

So we just gonna put our murder game down on everybody in the city that's not apart of our team baby tells Bear, black, and Gooba as they stand in front of the house they just had a meeting in back of bruh we just talked about this black says cutting baby off from talking, man shut the fuck up baby replied Yo y'all need to chill out we all together Bear says coming to black rescue y'all funny is hell Gooba adds to the conversation, Black stands their shooting Baby 50 to life one day I'm a kill you're ass for all ways tryna diss me that's my word black says to himself in his head.

DOLLAR, CASH & TONE

Cash pull your mask down Dollar tells him while they lean against the wall of the corner store wall, man I want these nigga's to know it was me fuck this mask Cash says while taken the mask off his head and throwing it on the ground, cash you're being real dumb right now pick that mask up and put it on Tone tells Cash, man fuck that shit cash says right before he bends the corner with his mac-11 out and opens fire on the block, fuck Tone says following behind Cash opening fire also right behind Cash.

BEAR, BLACK, GOOBA, & BABY

So we gonna find the nigga Shorty and get some cars from him? Gooba asked man he not the only nigga who knows how to steal cars, we got lil bruhs that know how to steal cars to Bear replies, Bear would hate to go through Shorty for anything at all I'm saying sin do be having some nice fast cars Baby say oh shit watch out Black yells pushing Bear to the ground right before the shots ring off Boom, boom, boom, boc, boc, boc, boc, boc, the machine guns ring off like it's the fourth of july boom, boom, boom, boom, I'm hit black says right before he falls to the ground, everybody runs pass black trying to get away from the shooters, just before black eyes shut he sees a person standing over him who turns out to be his cousin baby they lock eyes for a minute and then black life leaves him, baby tries to black lifeless body up from the ground as the shots still ring off Bloc, bloc, bloc, black is not the only body lifeless on the block two little homies are also dead before everybody made it to the middle of the block.

TONE, CASH, DOLLAR, & SHORTY

Go, go, Tone yells as they jumped back into the stolen hemI cherokee, oh shit Newark Dollar says spotting a black and while Newark police car coming to a stop at the light on 19th st and 18th ave, go cash yells from the back seat, and Shorty takes off down 18th ave speeding pass the police car which takes off right behind them, Tone looks behind them and the police car is not even a block away, yo go Tone yells, yo chill out let him do his thing Dollar says as he turns up the radio and yo-gotti january 10 cd plays Dollar turn the radio music up to full max, so Shorty can zone out and do his thing without hearing everybody yelling which way to turn, which would only make him more nervous than he already is, as Shorty gets to the light on 18th ave and Grove st with ease he breaks down and busts a right turn onto Grove st the police does the same Coming pass Grove st school Shorty notice two state police cars trying to block his way of making a right turn, Shorty shakes the jeep towards the two police cars to scare them up just in-case they got the idea to try and ram the jeep as he shot pass them, as Shorty pass them they also join the chase making it now 3 police cars behind them now, as Shorty and his passengers approach Grove st and 14th ave Shorty busts a left turn down 14th ave heading towards speedway, once on speedway Shorty busts a right turn at full speed, bloc, bloc, bloc oh shit they shooting at us Tone yells out while ducking down in the back seat, Shorty doesn't hear nothing Tone says he's zoned out with yo-gotti rappin about real niggas Shorty feels as yo-gotti is talking straight to him, Shorty gets on the parkway entrance without a problem not even slowing down Boom, boom, the back window falls out due to the shots from the police, yo I'm about to bust back at them cash says lifting his mac 11 up from laying on the seat, nah chill out Tone says while grabbing cash arm stopping him from shooting at the police, man they gonna fuck around and kill us if we don't back them down cash replied

Snatching his arm away from, dolla just sits back in his own zone, what's going on in Dollar mind is the years they gonna be sitting in the county jail for if they get caught tonight, for Shorty he continues to do his thing dipping in and outta traffic trying to shake the police cars behind them, bloc, bloc, bloc, cash mac 11 sounds off as he tries to back the police cars up off them while they exit the parkway in nutley New Jersey, doing 120mph the jeep swerves a little but Shorty puts it right back under control slowing the hemi down and making a blind left turn at the red light damn near getting the back off the jeep smashed in by a passing car, bloc, bloc, bloc bloc, bloc, cash lets off a few more shots to back the police cars more so they can't see the next left turn they take, so they could jump back on the parkway going south back toward Newark, you got em you got em Tone tells Shorty while looking behind them at the police cars falling back, we good now cash says as they approach the toll booth, oh shit watch out Tone yells as he seed a man on the side of the highway holding something in his hand pointing it towards the jeep Boom, boom, boom the shots from the police officer on the side of the road rocks the stolen jeep side to side as they hits the jeep, lucky no one gets shot, go, go Tone yells bloc, bloc, bloc the shot sound off from cash mac as he shoots out the back window at the police officer who shot at them you got em jump off in East Orange we gotta bail outta this shit Tone says as Shorty does the max speed limit on the jeep which is 140 mph leaving the police cars behind them for good get off right here Tone yells to Shorty who gets off the parkway going a little to fast for the jeep which starts to swerve too much catch it catch it cash yells but the hemi loses control and crashes into someones driveway and into a park car now the race is off and it's every man for himself with everybody running their own way.

THE NEXT DAY BH

BH pardon myself you don't mind me calling you BH do you? Not at all BH replied well BH my name is James Gray and I'm head of the prosecutor office, and from my understanding you called the office wishing to talk to somebody from the office, Mr.Gray say yeah I did I have a lot of information that I'm willing to give up for my freedom back BH replied Mr.Gray is shock by this news because he did his homework on BH before he came to see him today, and what he learned was BH was suppose to be a stand up nigga and AJ best friend, but nowadays no one is safe a dude would tell on his own mother and that's a true statement because some people really ratted on their mother's BH listen to because I'm not gonna bull shit you, you're in some deep shit the charges you have against you hold a lot of time unless you got some good stuff meaning murders carjacking robberies things of that nature Mr.Gray tells him I could tell you about so much stuff you'll think I was lying BH replied well I got this recorder I'm a set it up and all you gotta do is talk Mr.Gray replied Nah I'm not talking until we make some kind of deal BH say well I'm the man you need to talk to about that so what are you looking for outta cooperating? Mr.Gray asked I want outta this place for one then I wanna be place in a witness protection program and last I want my daughter BH requests ok let me go to the office and type up our agreement and I'll be back within two hours but when I come back I'll have the state police with me are you ok with that? Mr.Gray say I'll be waiting it's not like I'm going anywhere BH replied Ms. Roosevelt lets go Mr.Gray tells his second in command.

TOMMY & BIG DAWG

Bruh good looking with opening the store up for me this morning Big-dawg tells Tommy as he walked into their sneaker store, I wasn't doing nothing anyway so why not Tommy replied, while putting 200 dollars in small bills in the cash register, man the little chick that I had with me last night act like she ain't wanna go home this morning I had to damn near beg the little bitch to leave Big-dawg tells Tommy while shaking his head at the situation he had this morning, don't tell me you took the thot to your house? Tommy asked hoping Big-dawg didn't do that bruh I already know the shit but I didn't feel like jumping on 1&9 to find no hotels It was kind of late when she called me, Big-dawg replied bruh you slipping Tommy tells Big-dawg upset that he's being loose by taking a hood rat to where he rest his head at. Ayo did you ever call your father about Na-jay situation? Big-dawg ask trying to change the subject, nah he ain't answer the phone for me you know me and him haven't been talking due to the situation over AJ Tommy say yo y'all buggin beefing over a nigga, at the end of the day that's you're father job you need to understand that, I'm about to call him now myself Big-dawg says while taking out his cell phone to call Det.Jackson.

DET. JACKSON

Hello? Hey pops what's good? Who this? Det.Jackson asked due to him not looking at the caller id on his phone, it's dawg pops Big-dawg tells him over the other end of the phone, hold on Det.Jackson says while pushing Hazel arm from across his chest and getting outta the bed, once inside the bed-room half bath-room Det.Jackson asks into the phone what do you want boy? It's my day off today I'm trying to rest Det.Jackson tells Big-dawg, alright I'm a make it quick than, me and Tommy tryna find out about one of our peoples we wanna know if you heard anything about his situation Big-dawg say ok what's his name hold, hold, didn't I tell y'all I was done doing shit like this? Det. Jackson asks yeah I know I'm sorry about it but this is our mans pops Big-dawg replies and looks to Tommy who shakes his head because he knew his father was gonna say this, yeah just like that last guy was y'all mans but whats this ass hole name? Det.Jackson asks He goes by Na-jay Big-dawg say What? Det.Jackson yells into the phone, I really think you two wanna go to fucking jail and I'm a tell you both, I'm not going with y'all but for this Na-jay guy he's going down and away for a long time and if you don't wanna go to jail with him than stay the fuck away from him Det.Jackson tells them before hanging up the phone, these two are the dumbest drug dealers I know Det. Jackson says to himself, Det.Jackson phone starts to ring again in his hand What? the fuck do y'all want now Det.Jackson asked into the phone, hold partner it's me Det.Killburg replied, oh pardon me Det. Jackson tells him, well it's ok but I'll be at your house to get you in 15 minutes I just dropped Vickie off at home, it's our day off today what are you talking about? Det.Jackson asked, well last night the city had three murder's which lead to a high speed chase with Newark police and the state police a few shots were let go by the police and the suspects at each other the suspects cashed in East Orange New Jersey Det.Killburg tells him, well did they catch any of them Det. Jackson asked, hell know you know Newark police and the state boys can't drive, but the driver of the stole car is dead for the most part the Lt White wants us at the scene Det.Killburg says well you said it was three murders where are the other two located at? Det.Jackson asked everything started on 18th st and 18th ave just be ready when I get their I'll fill you in on everything when we get together Det.Killburg tells Det.Jackson before ending the call and where you're supposed to be going? Hazel asked while walking into the bathroom naked catching the end of Det.Jackson and his partner conversation, I gotta go on the clock but I want you to stay here until I get back Det.Jackson tells her while she sits on the toilet using the bathroom with know regard to Det.Jackson being in the bath-room I'll be here just hurry up back here Hazel replied, damn why couldn't Tommy mother been a little understanding like her Det.Jackson asks himself.

AJ

So Mr. Boss you'll be release tonight from my understanding, and you don't have know holds on you AJ lawyer ty tells him, yo you're the best I owe you lunch for this one AJ tells her, don't make know promises you not gonna keep ty replied, truly looking forward to AJ taken her out lunch, through all the years she's been AJ lawyer this is the first time he ever needed her for himself all the other times he called on her was for her to represent one of the little homies needing a lawyer, I'm a man of my word I got you just when I call you be ready AJ replies ok mr boss we'll see ty tells him while grabbing up all the paperwork that they were going through on the table of the attorney and inmate visit room.

SNAP, BARK, & SKY

Sky I hope this the right house? Bark says as they walk inside the house looking around at all the expenses stuff around the house, fool I know where I slept at last night sky says while leading the way towards the bed-room, look lets just hurry up before the nigga get back home because I'm not gonna play around with him, I'm a light his ass right up with this mac-90 Snap says watching their backs as he holds them down with the machine gun, I hope we find something in here because bnez are not my thing Bark says sizing up the 60 inch tv on the wall man flip this bitch upside down and lets get the fuck outta here before West Orange police show up Snap tells them as they start searching Big-dawg house.

NA-JAY & TOMMY

Nah that shit ain't have nothing to do with me Na-jay tells Tommy as he watches eyewitness news about the killings that happen on 18th st and 18th ave, bruh good looking with calling you're people for me it's cool that he couldn't come through and help me out Na-jay says jumping back to the conversation they just had before Tommy asked him did he have something to do with the killings last night Just lay low and if I could help you with anything else let me know Tommy tells him bruh all I need you to do is keep hitting me with this dope so I could have my money up whenever they catch me, Na-jay replied I got you just hit me when you need more work Tommy tells him Aight I got you Na-jay replied before ending the call so what we gonna do now? Lisa asked once Na-jay was off the phone, we gonna have him give us a few thousand bricks than we're gonna hit the road fuck Newark we going to another state and turn that shit out and turn everybody phantom out that bitch Na-jay tells her.

GOOBA, BABY & BEAR

Yo that's fucked up what happen to black last night Gooba says to Baby and Bear as they stand on 21st and Roosevelt word up bruh was a good dude Bear replied man fuck all this sad shit we gotta put on for the bruh Bear says all in his feelings, bruh you sound crazy right now how we gonna put it in on somebody and we don't even know where this shot coming from baby replied Yo you think this shit coming from the same people that hit the Old-man up Gooba asked, bruh it might just be baby replied, we need to holla at AJ and see what he thinks about it or if he know something about who might be moving out on us Bear says making sense for the first time I'm about to call him now Bear says as he watches the robbery and homicide police car slow roll pass them.

TONE, CASH & DOLLAR

Cash did you get threw to your cousin phone yet? Tone asked walking back into the living room from just using the bathroom nah his shit going right to voicemail still Cash replied yo I hope he got away last night because I'm not trying to go to jail Dollar say bruh if my cousin did get caught he's not gonna rat on us it ain't know snitch in my dna Cash say taking up for Shorty and the rest of his family unbeknown to them is once they crashed Shorty ran two blocks away from the scene and fell out behind someone's garage where he slowly died due to internal bleeding and his lungs both failing, the only way Shorty made it two blocks away was he scared outta his life.

JJ & ZOE UMD, N.J

Your old ass need to stop playing and wake up because I'm tired of keep coming here seeing you laid up like some sucker ass nigga JJ says to the unconscious man who lays in the hospital bed hearing all that JJ has just said but can't seem to find the power to open his eye's bay can I ask you a question? Zoe asked JJ sitting in another chair inside the hospital room, go head JJ tells her with his eyes still on the unconscious man, why do y'all call him the old man? He doesn't look like a old man to me Zoe say baby once he stops being a punk an wakes up he'll be able to answer your question for himself JJ replied, how about I answer her question after I'm done beating your ass for calling me outta my name all these days the old man says in an weak voice oh shit your up JJ yells baby go get the nurse JJ yells at Zoe while rushing to the side of the old man bed.

VICKIE & HAZEL

So your really gonna sit up in his house all day waiting for him to get off work, it sound to me like somebody giving up their hoe card Vickie says to Hazel as they sit inside Jo hair salon on 16th ave and 12th st hoe card? I never knew I had one of thoses and for your information I really do like Tom alot I could see me and him going far in life Hazel says as she starts to day dream, damn bitch he truly got your ass open? but fuck all that can you believe that the old man from homebase not dead Vickie says out loud so other customers could here their conversation and Vickie could get some attention that's crazy right? and all these mother fuckers thinks he's dead Hazel replieds the shop is now quiet all eyes are on Vickie and Hazel and all ears open Lisa, Erica and Lady-red can't believe their ears they knew for sure that they killed the old man all the shots they put into that little bmw jeep it's no way he's alive but from what they are hearing he's truly alive, I guess when you got county Det.'s as a boy friends you get all the real information and not the washed up tmz hood news Vickie say ain't that right Hazel adds Tommy little sister Ashley just so happens to be getting her hair done today at the shop also Ashley had the chance of meeting the old man at the house she shares with her brother so she knows who he is Ashley slide out her iphone and texts Tommy to let him know about the two county Det.'s these hoes claim to be their man because from her understanding her father and his partner are the only two county Det.'s of Essex county his job is the reason he never have time to spend with Ashley.

SNAP, BARK & SKY

Yo I'm a ask you one more time where the fuck is the work at? Snap questions Big-dawg before slapping him again as Big-dawg sits tied up to one of his own chairs inside his house, Big-dawg feels like a jackass right now he wishes he never brought Sky to his house, while at the sneaker store Big-dawg got a call from his little mans Mike who is Na-jay little cousin claiming he needed a few bricks of dope, he told Big-dawg that Na-jay didn't feel like coming outside at the time and the girls were out getting their hair done so they couldn't bring it to him and the block was jumping, so Big-dawg got in his car and headed home once he got to his house, he notice a old body tinted loose Audi S4 that he never saw before parked in front of his house, Big-dawg by pass the car thinking it just might be his neighbors family member car, but Snap little brother sat behind the wheel of the stolen car, once Big-dawg pulled up and made his way to the front door, Snap little brother called Snap and put him on point, Snap first thought was to get low, but than he came up with the idea for them to hide and once Big-dawg made it in the house they were all to rush him and tie him up, bruh, bruh we could do this shit all day it's not like I got anywhere to be, but I'm a tell you like this if you don't tell me where that cash at I'm a say fuck it and push you're shit back Snap tells Big-dawg while putting the mac 90 in his face letting him know he means business, bruh his phone ringing again Bark tells Snap, man fuck his phone Snap replied looking into Big-dawg eye's, from the ringtone that sounds off the phone let's Big-dawg know it's Tommy calling, this is now the tenth time Tommy called him, it's like Tommy knows something is not right or Tommy himself is in some trouble also, fuck it the cash and the work is inside the refrigerator Big-dawg tells Snap, hoping that they'll just hurry up and take the work so he could see what's good? With Tommy, fuck why didn't I think of that shit in the first place, that's some fat boy shit you did placing it in the refrigerator but I'll remember that info next time I'm robbing another fat nigga Snap tells Big-dawg, yo bruh it's the mother load in here Bark yells from the kitchen, once Big-dawg said where the cash and the work was at Bark and Sky took off to go check it out, Snap come look at this shit Sky yells to him, Snap looks at Big-dawg than takes off towards the kitchen, once inside the kitchen Snap is surprise once he sees all the work and money that Bark has already sitting on the floor and still taking out the refrigerator, we hit big bruh Bark says reaching back inside the refrigerator to take out some more work or money so what we gonna do about him in their Sky asks Snap talking about Big-dawg, I'm about to handle him right now Snap replied before walking back toward the living room, yo what the fuck you think you doing? Snap ask Big-dawg catching him trying to get free from the chair that he tied him down in, nothing Big-dawg replied, well dig bruh good looking for the come up but I gotta kill you but I'm a let you pick if you want a close casket or not Snap tells him, come on lil bruh I gave you a blessing just take all the work and the money and go Big-dawg pleas to Snap, that's not what I asked you Snap replied while aiming the mac-90 at Big-dawg face letting him know his time is up on this earth, man fuck you suck my dick Big-dawg says bloc, bloc, bloc, three shots sound off from the mac-90 opening Big-dawg face up, yo what the fuck? Bark says running into the living room to see what was going on, man just go grab all the shit and let's get the fuck outta here before the police get here Snap tells him while looking at Big-dawg life less body.

DET. JACKSON, DET. KILLBURG & PETE

This is how things are gonna work out due to Na-jay still being on the street's you're good he can't find out you told on him until he gets caught and gets his paperwork, and what the D.A office just called us and said is the feds might be looking to charge him with the Rico due to his gang dealings Det.Killburg tells Pete, I understand all that but I know it's gonna be hard for me to get in touch with Na-jay things just don't work that easy Pete tells them hoping they understand, well take your time we're not rushing you just take this cell phone ir's tap already and whenever you find out any reliable information call us our numbers are already in the phone, Det.Jackson tells Pete, ok can I go now Pete asks ready to get outta the police station, yeah go head Det.Killburg says, damn I hope that kid doesn't get himself killed Det.Jackson says after Pete left the room, he'll be alright Det.Killburg replies but could really careless if Pete get killed or not.

LATER ON THAT DAY UMD, N.J

Damn Black really dead AJ asks, yeah bruh gone Baby replied as JJ holds his cell phone while they all talk to AJ and Krazy J on speaker, don't worry about it, you and bruh would be home tonight I know I could count on y'all to handle thing's until I get back on my feet the old man tells AJ I'll tell you like this somebody gonna die tonight if they let us out tonight Krazy J tells them, bruh we're gonna be waiting for y'all Bear let's AJ and his brother know, ayo why the jail on lock down? JJ asked AJ trying to change the subject so they could stop talking so reckless over the phones, man the nigga Na-jay bitch ass put the green light on all tp nigga's AJ replied as soon as AJ said that Bear think he catches on to the problems at hand, yo you think Na-jay the one behind all this shit? Bear asks everyone Bear you might just be right the old man tells Bear, now that you brought it up I think so to AJ tells him also, word up! Krazy J agreed, I'm a kill that nigga Baby says real emotional, well that settles it it's on sight AJ tells them ending the call y'all heard him it's on sight the old man tells them and they all start to leave outta the hospital room after dabbing the old man up, all but JJ and Zoe bruh I know thoses my brother's but Before JJ could say anything else the old man cuts him off, lil bruh ride with them they hand picked by me myself the old man tells JJ Say less JJ replied before making his way outta the hospital room behind his homie's Hold JJ the old man calls him stopping him in his tracks, what's good? Big bruh JJ ask With only murder on his mind What's the deal with her right their? the old man asks pointing at Zoe She my wife and she's now tp JJ tells him which let's the old man know where Zoe stands Aight cool welcome to the family the old man tells Zoe Thanks you for accepting in me Zoe replied happy that the old man accepted her into the family and Zoe I'll let you know why I'm the old man once I'm outta here the old man tells her and closes his eyes to get some much needed rest Let's go JJ tells Zoe taking her by the hand.

TOMMY, NA-JAY 1&9 CAR-LOT

Na my people's said she was getting her hair done today at some hair shop and she overheard some chicks talking about the old man not dead, fuck Na-jay says to himself, Na-jay didn't plan on Tommy hearing about the news so fast Na-jay was hoping he'll be long gone before Tommy found out the news but that just goes to show you people love to run their mouth in Newark, burh it's know way he could be alive after all them shots we put into that jeep it's know way Na-jay tells him shaking his head, Na I hope you're right and my lil people's just might of heard wrong Tommy replies hoping the news his little sister Ashley told him not right but why do you need 5,000 bricks? I just hit you with 3,000 bricks not to long ago Tommy says yeah I know bruh but I got a sell for 2,000 bricks to my little homies outta state and I need my regular 3,000 bricks because, I'm low Na-jay replies aight I got you, you got most of the money for the last 3,000 bricks on you now? Tommy asked come on Tommy I'm not dumb, if you forgot I'm on the run why would I move around with all that money, and take the chance of the police pulling us over and bagging me with your money If that was to happen at least you could still get your money Na-jay says making his story sound good, which he knows Tommy is gonna buy, because he's not putting Tommy money at risk that's sounds about right, but bruh I'm not gonna lie I don't be fronting out this much shit to know body but I'm a give it to you Tommy says and reaches into his GL550 benz truck for the gym bag which is filled up with the 5,000 bricks of dope Na-jay asked for aight I'm a come through tonight and pick up that money from you but I gotta find this fool Big-dawg he haven't been answering his phone Tommy says handing the gym bag over to Na-jay you think he locked up? Na-jay asked while looking into the gym bag at all the bricks of dope If he got locked up I'll know Tommy says and thinks about his father aight later Na-jay tells Tommy no doubt Tommy replied turning his back to Na-jay get into his benz truck which was the worse thing he could have done Boom Boom Boom Boom the four shots to the back from the 357 knocks Tommy face down on the ground Na-jay runs up on Tommy and finish the job off Boom Boom the two shots to the back of the head let's Na-jay know Tommy is done Na-jay takes off to the awaiting bmw x5M truck which Lisa Erica and Lady-red sits inside of waiting for his return damn it took you long enough Erica says once Na-jay gets inside the truck you got it Lady-red asked once Na-jay is inside the truck Yeah pull off Na-jay tells her hold on we forgot something Erica tells him what? Na-jay asked this Boom Boom the two shots kill Na-jay damn bitch push his ass out the Lisa says from the front seat He's out now go Erica tells Lady-red who takes off leaving two dead body's behind them Where to now ladies? Lady-red asks It don't it's our turn to run shit Lisa replies for Na-jay he didn't even see this coming everybody thinks you could trust females nowadays but they be the most disloyal ones in the game.

AJ & KRAZY J

Bruh I thought the lawyer said we'll be outta here tonight Krazy J asks his brother while looking out the small cell window that's what she told me but they might be letting us go in the morning AJ tells his little brother man I knew it was too good to be true Krazy J says real sad little bruh stop doubting it our bail paid you know this county dumb is hell AJ tells him Aight I'm just gonna watch tv Krazy J replies.

V-NASTY HOUSE 4:30 AM THE NEXT MORNING

Boom the loud noise wakes up everybody inside the house what the fuck was that Kintahe asks getting outta the bed he shares with his wife get on the fucking floor now the police officer's yell as they run into each room holding machine guns while dress in all black have y'all lost y'all fucking minds get the fuck out my house V-nasty yells at the police officers while getting out the bed a little to fast for the police liking which turned out to be a big mistake the police takes her right to the ground pinning her with a knee in her back I'm a sue all you mother fucker's I promise y'all that V-nasty say well you're gonna be doing that right from your jail cell one of the police officers replied Ma ma Qwae-ma yells from her bed room It's ok baby just do ass these crackers say V-nasty yells back to her we got a fighter in here one of the police officers yell out to the other officers trying to get them to come help him fight Bar-man off who's punching him and putting up a big fight y'all some pussy's why y'all gotta jump me Bar-man says still trying his best to fight the cop's If y'all hurt my baby I'm a kill y'all crackers V-nasty says while laying on the floor that's another charge for you miss a cop tells V-nasty Miss this dick V-nasty replied.

KIM

Please don't hurt me Kim says while holding her son in her arms Miss we're gonna ask you to stand up slowly and if you cooperate this will be over with quick we're not robbers or murderers we're police officers the mask man tells Kim showing her his badge This puts Kim at ease a little now that she knows that they are not in her house to kill her can I ask you why are y'all kick in my door scaring me and my son? Kim asks well we have a know knock search warrant the officer tells Kim showing her the paperwork Once Kim heard the words search warrant she passed out with lil AJ still in her arms Kim knows once these people flipped the house they were gonna find all AJ guns in the basement and being as AJ wasn't there to claim the guns she'll be wearing them.

9:37 AM UMD, N.J

Mr.Rich wake up Prosecutor James Gray tells the old man calling him by his first name waking him up outta his sleep man I already told y'all I don't know who shot me the Old-man replies oh that's why you think I'm here? Mr.Gray asks the old man wakes up fully now so what do you want? the old man asked well I just wanted to meet you myself because I heard so much about but long story short I'm the head prosecutor in essex county and I'm here to read you your rights and charges you are now under arrest for two counts of murder, 5 gun charges the Rico which is my favorite drugs which we founded in you're house and a shit load of money I guess what they says about you is true Mr.Gray say the old man can't believe his ears, not only did he get shot and his wife get killed but now he's going to jail also fuck it what are you waiting for then arrest me the old man says sticking out his arms so he could be handcuff I'll be please to do the honors prosecutor Gray says while handcuffing the old man who still lays in the hospital bed.

AJ & KRAZY J

They called both of us out for attorney visits this can't be good Krazy J says as he and his brother walks off the locked down unit to see their lawyers you both can come in this room together AJ lawyer ty tells the brothers with her head sticking out of the attorney and inmate visit room Once AJ and Krazy J are both inside the room Ty takes over the meeting look we don't have much time they have y'all mother, sister, brother, and you're mother husband at the prosecutor office the claim to have found 18 million dollars in cash and two guns at you're mother house AJ and Krazy J both look at each other, they both know that the lawyer isn't lying because when they last counted the money at their mother house it was a little over 18 million dollars the police must had help their self to a little bit of the cash and the two guns AJ bought for his mother house in case anybody ever tried to rob them AJ and Krazy J also showed the house hold how to shoot the 357's and AJ they also have your wife they also claim to have founded 350,000 dollars in cash and multiple guns in her house Ty tells them both but like I stated before they have them all at the prosecutor office and from what they are telling us is they want you two to claim ownership of the money and the guns and they'll let your love ones go also with you two doing that you won't be able to make bail any longer Ty tells them I fucking told you it was to good to be true, I knew they weren't gonna let us out on bail Krazy J say hold on bruh, Ty why did they wait until now to run in our peoples homes, what's the reason behind this? AJ asked trying to get a understanding on what's going on what Ty forgot to tell you both is you're co-de Lee cold turned state on you two and also on a Mr.Rich something, Miss.Dutch, Krazy J lawyer tells them this news just shook Krazy J and AJ world alright tell them it's all mines Krazy J tells the lawyers nah lil bruh chill AJ tells him nah it's because I got him popped that he turned state Krazy J replied bruh it was in him to be a rat AJ tells Krazy J well AJ I think you're both not understanding what I told y'all they want you both to take the rap to cut your love ones free Ty tells them what we gonna do? Krazy J asked the only thing we could do we'll do it AJ says talking for the both of them ok I'll make the call now Miss.Dutch says leaving out the room AJ I'm so sorry Ty tells him while breaking down crying, due to AJ new situation bruh we lived a good life Krazy J says also breaking down crying bruh it's not over I got a plan AJ replies I'm all ears Krazy J says me to Ty adds look we're about to switch …